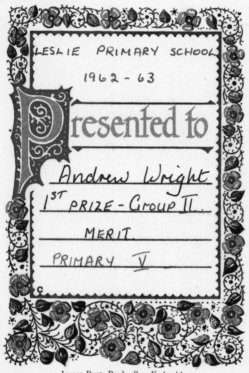

LESLIE PRIMARY SCHOOL
1962 - 63

Presented to

Andrew Wright

1ST PRIZE - Group II.

MERIT.

PRIMARY V

James Burt, Bookseller, Kirkcaldy.

SNOW ON THE WOLD

What this story is about:

Driving down from London to a remote Cotswold village where he was to spend a few days with an old school friend, Brian Carter pulled up sharply to avoid something lying in the road.

The excitement aroused in the village by the subsequent police investigations soon subsided, but Brian's friend Frank, on leave from Scotland Yard, suspected that the incident was of more than local significance. The appearance in the neighbourhood of a man known to have a criminal record confirmed his suspicions. Clearly a local resident was at the head of a country-wide organisation of crooks. At the same time stories were told of figures seen on moonlit nights near the ancient burial mound on Black Knapp. After an accident forced Frank to keep to the house, Brian set himself to track down the criminals, and a lonely vigil on the snow-covered hillside led to surprising revelations.

BRIAN WRENCHED THE STEARING WHEEL OVER

Snow on the Wold   (p.84

SNOW ON THE WOLD

WILFRID ROBERTSON

FREDERICK WARNE & CO. LTD

LONDON AND NEW YORK

Printed in Great Britain

CONTENTS

CHAPTER I

WHAT LAY IN THE ROAD

THE winter day had been wet when Brian Carter left London. But as he passed through Oxford, heading north-westwards in the small second-hand car he had saved up to buy, the sky began to show signs of clearing and blue patches appeared between the drifting clouds.

As Brian drove onwards he turned over in his mind what had led up to his present journey. He and Frank Tilney had become friends in their schooldays, but the need to earn their livings had parted them. Brian had gone into a London office and Frank had joined the police, about which he had always been keen. For a while they had written to each other; then suddenly Brian's letters had remained unanswered, and the two had lost touch completely.

Then, to Brian's surprise, the long silence had been broken. Frank Tilney had written from an address in the Cotswolds, saying he was on extended leave and inviting Brian to come down for a visit. He had added that he felt very guilty about

7

not answering those letters in the past, but there had been a reason which he would explain when they met again. He said nothing, however, about how he came to be in that unexpected locality, nor if he were putting up at this place alone or staying with some friend.

Brian had promptly decided to accept the invitation if he could obtain leave of absence. He had met with no difficulty there, for business was slack at the time and he was due for a holiday anyway.

After leaving Oxford, the countryside through which Brian drove changed steadily in character. It became more undulating. The villages were no longer built of brick but of grey Cotswold stone, and hedgerows rapidly gave place to loosely constructed walls of the same material. The switchback of the wolds grew more pronounced; alternately he dropped into valleys and climbed rolling crests which, now that the rain had passed away, were gilded on their western sides by the winter afternoon's sun.

On the next brow Brian pulled up to consult his road-map. According to Frank's letter, Kinford was the nearest village, and the contours showed that it was close to where the high Cotswold drops abruptly to the level flats that stretch westward to the Severn and are known as the Vale of Evesham. Brian saw that to reach his destination he must shortly turn off the more frequented road and take what was obviously a winding country lane.

Weathered lettering on a signpost gave him his cue. After following a narrow road for a couple of miles he saw ahead a cluster of grey stone cottages that must be the village of Kinford. On reaching it he would stop and ask the way to where Frank was living.

He was to stop before then, however. As he rounded a sharp curve some two or three hundred yards short of the village, he saw a human figure lying sprawled on its face in the middle of the road.

Brian jammed on the brakes and pulled up. He jumped out of the car and hurried forward. With a shock he realised that the man was dead.

For a moment Brian considered what he had better do. Apparently the fellow had been knocked down by some hit-and-run car. The police ought to be informed. Was the village just ahead large enough to have a resident constable? He had better go on and find out—if not, there would probably be a telephone call-box. Meanwhile he must shift the body out of the way; half lifting it, he dragged it over to the grass verge, and then returning to his car he hastened on to the village.

He found the local bobby easily enough, for he caught sight of him strolling along the village street on his way back from his morning round. The bored look disappeared from the constable's face when Brian stopped and reported what he had found.

"Wasn't you who ran over him by any chance?" demanded P.C. Watts as he felt for his little-used notebook.

Brian said it was not.

"Then who might you be, and where are you goin'?"

Brian told him. "I suggest that I turn the car round and take you back to where I found the chap," he added.

"Ah." P.C. Watts climbed in, knocking his helmet over his nose as he hit it against the low roof. He took it off, made sure that it was not dented, and placed it carefully on his bent knees.

"I suppose you ent touched this body?" he went on as Brian drove back the way he had come.

"No, beyond moving it to the side of the road."

"Shouldn't ha' done that," said Watts, shaking his head.

"What should I have done—driven over him?" asked Brian in retort. "The road's narrow, and he was lying in the middle of it."

"Well maybe it couldn't be helped," the constable conceded as Brian slowed and stopped the car.

P.C. Watts bent over the body. "Why, I know this chap!" he said as he straightened himself.

"Name o' Romsey. Works as a manservant to Mr. Lethwick over yonder." He pointed to a new-looking house standing some little distance back from the road—a somewhat aggressive type of building that might not be noticeable in a suburb but seemed out of place in contrast with the old stone cottages of the nearby village.

"Would you like me to go up there and tell this poor chap's employer?" asked Brian.

The constable shook his head. "That had best bide till later. Right now my sergeant ought to be told, and a doctor and an ambulance fetched. But by rights this didn't ought to be left. If I stay here will you go back to the village and ring up? There's a call-box up the street." He added the required number.

"Certainly I will. After which I suppose I can carry on? You know where I'm going, and my friend's expecting me."

P.C. Watts studied Brian for a moment, and apparently came to the conclusion that he looked honest.

"O.K., seein' you're stoppin' with Mr. Tilney who's livin' up the slad. But you'll be wanted later, y'understand, seein' you found this chap. There'll be an inquest."

Brian nodded. As he was about to re-enter his

car he remembered he did not know where Frank was staying, and turned to ask the way.

"Go along the village street and past the 'Rising Sun'," he was told. "Twenty yards beyond the inn there's a turn to the left. Take it, and keep on up the slad. That road don't go nowhere else, so you can't go wrong."

Brian drove off. He made the required 'phone-call and then took the turn beyond the village inn. He had no idea what a slad was, but he guessed that it must be the local term for the shallow valley in which he presently found himself.

He splashed onwards through the puddles that pitted the rough track. At the point where it ceased to be a road at all, and became a field trail, stood what was presumably his destination—a cottage among some trees, with indications of outbuildings and a garden at the back.

The sound of his car had been heard. As Brian drew up, Frank Tilney appeared at the cottage door and came forward with a welcoming wave of his hand. "So you've found your way all right!" he called. "I was beginning to wonder whether you'd missed it."

At the first glance Brian saw little change in his friend since last they had met; it was much the same tall fair-haired figure he remembered. But as they shook hands he noticed the look of weariness and strain in the blue eyes.   He guessed that Frank had either been ill or undergoing considerable nervous tension, which would account for his being given long leave from his job.

"I didn't hurry," Brian replied.   "Besides, I got delayed just as I was nearing this village of yours." In a few words he told of his discovery in the lane and the fetching of the village constable.

"That's queer," commented Frank.   "If it had been on a main road, with fools blinding along at high speeds, it would be understandable.   But there's very little traffic on these lanes beyond an occasional farmer's lorry or tradesman's van.   I suppose he *had* been knocked down by a car, and not collapsed from a heart-attack or something?"

"There was the muddy mark of a tyre on his clothes.   Your local bobby saw it too."

"Was it anyone he knew?"

"He did mention a name—Romsey I think it was."

"Romsey?   The fellow who works for Lethwick?"

"Yes, that's right.   The bobby mentioned that name too."

"Oh well——" Frank shrugged as if he could say more but had decided not to.   "Come along in," he went on.   "Leave your car where it is for the present—we'll put it away later."   As the two moved towards the house he added, "I don't know

2

whether I told you in my letter—I had this cottage lent to me for my leave, and a motherly dame from the village, Mrs. Pratley by name, comes up daily to look after us."

"Us?" queried Brian, noting the plural.

"Yes. Pamela's here with me. You remember her, surely?"

It took Brian a moment before he did. Then a recollection of Frank's young sister, a rather plain child whom he had met once or twice, came back to him. But that was years ago, and she would be getting quite grown up now.

Brian followed his friend into the sitting-room of the cottage. It was warm and cosy, and a bright fire burned in the hearth. As he crossed over to warm himself after his cold drive, a door at the other side of the room opened. A girl as tall as Frank, and with the same fair hair, entered. Brian guessed that this must be Pamela, though he would never have recognised her, for the plain kid had developed into a self-assured young woman. She came forward with a smile, holding out her hand.

"We have met before, though it's a long time ago," she said. "I expect you're dying for some tea after your journey. I'll get it as soon as I can; seeing to tea is always my job, as the good lady who comes from the village to housekeep for us goes home after lunch. In the meanwhile I'll leave Frank to entertain you."

"While we're waiting we might as well put away your car," suggested Frank. "Then we can come back to the fire and be comfortable."

Brian nodded agreement, and the two emerged again into the open. Under Frank's directions Brian drove round to the back by way of a field-gate that hung on sagging hinges. A shed stood invitingly open, into which he ran the car, parking it alongside another which obviously belonged to his host. As he had guessed when approaching by the road, there was a fairly large, though much neglected, garden and orchard at the back of the cottage. Among the unpruned apple-trees rose a round tower-like structure of grey stone.

"What's that?" asked Brian as he helped to close the heavy door of the shed. "Looks like a sort of fortress, with those loopholes high up and no windows."

"Yes, it does, rather," Frank agreed. "Actually it's an ancient dovecot. This ground used to belong to the Manor once, I believe." He pointed to where the roof of a large house was visible among some trees nearly a mile away. "As you may know—but probably don't!—in the Middle Ages only lords of manors were allowed to keep large flocks of pigeons. Too destructive to crops, otherwise."

"Looks a queer old place."

"Yes. I'll show it to you tomorrow. There's a kind of storeroom below, and above it an upper chamber with nesting-boxes in the thickness of the walls. What you called loopholes were for the birds to go in and out—you can see the stone perching-ledges below each one. But meanwhile let's go back to the fire and some tea."

They found everything ready, and Pamela awaiting their return. As they ate and drank Brian spoke about his journey and gave his hostess an account of the discovery in the lane, about which he had already told Frank.

The girl asked for details, including the exact spot where the man had been found. Brian supplied them as best he could, siting the position by referring to the blatant new house nearby where, he understood, the victim had been employed.

"A repulsive-looking place!" commented Frank at this point. "Still, if it hadn't been for the Town and Country Planning people it would probably have been even more frightful and built of red brick. By all accounts, Lethwick's a retired businessman from London. I've run across him once or twice since I've been here, for he's always strolling round the village, cigar in mouth, telling the locals what fools they are. Not in so many words, but that's what it comes to. Naturally he's not exactly popular in Kinford."

"Nor was Romsey," put in Pamela. "I know it's not good form to say things about people who are dead," she went on to Brian, "but he was of the nosey type that village people can't stand. There won't be many tears shed for him in Kinford when the news gets round."

"Yes, a pair of them if it comes to that," commented Frank with a short laugh.

Talk drifted to other subjects, and though more than one opening occurred in which Frank might have spoken of what he had been doing, and why Brian had heard nothing of him for so long, he evaded them. Clearly he did not wish to discuss the subject at the moment.

When tea was over, Pamela rose to her feet. "I'll clear away these things and wash up," she said.

"Like me to come and give a hand?" volunteered Brian.

"No, no, you stop where you are and talk to Frank. You're going to be treated as a guest for to-night at least, though I may rope you in to-morrow!"

She disappeared with the loaded tray. Frank signed to Brian to take one of the armchairs by the fire, and seated himself in the other.

Brian was still keen to ask Frank for more details of what he had been doing since the two had last met, but it was obvious that his host did not intend to discuss the matter. Conversation turned to commonplace subjects. They talked of the past and of half-forgotten mutual acquaintances, and in due course went on to speak of their present surroundings. "You have certainly chosen a quiet spot for your holiday," remarked Brian at length.

"Yes, that's so," Frank agreed. "This is a real rural retreat and conditions are primitive. Though they have it at the village and the Manor, we've no electricity here, and we get our water-supply from a pump by the back door. Our only modern luxury is the telephone, which the owner who lent us the place had put in when he converted what was originally two tumble-down cottages."

Brian was about to speak again when the door opened and Pamela came in. "What, sitting in the dark?" she exclaimed. "Why didn't you light the lamp, Frank?"

"Oh, the firelight was sufficient. We were just talking."

"Well, now you'd better get on with some doing!" Pamela retorted briskly, taking a box of matches from the mantelpiece and tossing them to her brother. "Also, what about showing our guest to his room, instead of leaving me to do it? I've got to keep him up to the mark as a host!" she added to Brian with a laugh.

The evening passed pleasantly enough, but Brian was not sorry when the time came to go to bed, for he was tired after his long drive. As he changed into his pyjamas he wondered how he was going to enjoy his visit. It was fine renewing acquaintance with Frank, and from what he had seen of her, Pamela seemed a good sort; but he had a feeling that he might find things a bit boring before the end of his stay. He would have been surprised had he known how wrong this last estimate was to prove.

CHAPTER II

TWO MEN IN A TEA-SHOP

BRIAN was awakened by his door swinging open and the entrance of Frank. "Show a leg!" the intruder remarked. "It's not far off eight o'clock. Slept well?"

"Yes, rather!" replied Brian, sitting up and yawning.

"That's good. Here's some hot water." Frank dumped a battered enamelled jug on the floor. "Best we can do here. I told you things were primitive, and a bath will have to wait until the copper's heated up. Breakfast's nearly ready — Pamela's cooking it now, for Mrs. Pratley doesn't show up till about nine—so you'd better get a move on if you want any!"

Brian descended to find that Pamela had just brought in the meal. The three had hardly sat down to it when there was a loud rap at the back door.

"Who on earth's that?" exclaimed the girl, lowering her porridge spoon.

"Mrs. Pratley come early, perhaps," commented

her brother. "She wouldn't knock, though—she'd walk in. I expect it's old Nix wanting an early cuppa. That's your department, Pam. You'd better go and see."

"Oh bother. I suppose I had."

As the girl left the room Brian asked, "Who's Nix?"

"An old chap from the village who's doing a job for me. Part of one of the loose-stone walls round the orchard has collapsed, and he's the local expert at putting up these things. He's been at it for the last couple of days, so he should not be far off finishing." Frank turned his head as Pamela came back, and added, "Well, who was it?"

"You were right—it was Nix. He wants to see you about something, but won't say what. In fact he sounds quite mysterious."

"Well, he'll have to wait till I've finished breakfast," grumbled Frank, helping himself to bacon.

"I don't suppose he'll mind that, seeing you're paying him by the hour!" the girl retorted with a laugh as she sat down again.

When the meal was over, Frank got up. "Come along and let's see what the old chap wants," he said to Brian, who rose from his chair and followed.

Old Charlie, as Nix was usually known in the village, heaved himself up from the kitchen chair in which he had made himself comfortable while he waited.   He turned a weather-beaten face that had not been recently shaved towards his temporary employer.

"Mornin' to ye," he remarked, touching the battered cap which he had not thought it necessary to remove when he came in, and casting a glance of curiosity at Brian.

"Good morning. What's the trouble?" asked Frank.

"There ent no trouble in the manner o' speakin', but there might 'a' been, easy. You cummon an' look at this 'ere. Seen a lot o' rum things in my time."

"What is it, then?" Frank asked again.

Nix's only reply was to open the back door and step outside. The shambling figure, clad in garments whitened by stone-dust and greened by moss, led the way towards the place where he had been working.

The three reached the spot. The repairs were not far from being completed, and alongside lay the remainder of the stones that had not yet been replaced. Nix halted and turned.

"See them stones?" he asked, pointing to the dump. "Some on 'em what fell down ent no good to shove up agen. When I knocks off las' night I remembers there was some more layin' among them bushes back o' that there old dovecot. So time I gets 'ere 'smornin' I picks up me barrer and goes to fetch 'em.   Now you come along o' me."

Nix took the lead again.   A few yards short of the ancient building he paused dramatically and pointed.   In the middle of the track running through the grass under the apple trees was a hole about four feet across.   Beside it lay an overturned wheelbarrow and the spilt stones it had contained.

"I was a-wheelin' back that there barrer-load, and proper 'eavy it wor, too," Nix went on, "when I feels 'er start to sink, sudden-like.   I pulls back quick, I can tell ye!   Over goes me barrer, the 'andle ketchin' me leg and knockin' me off me feet.   I gets up, and when I looks—blow me! there was that 'ole!"

Frank and Brian moved forward to inspect.   It was clearly not a natural cavity but a circular man-made shaft, for it was lined with stone blocks, and portions of the rotting timber which had supported its covering of earth still projected round the rim.

"Looks like an old well or something," commented Brian.

"Ah.   Reckon you're right, mister.   Do ye know what?"   Nix indicated the hole with a gesture of his horny hand.   "Reckon it wor made 'underds o' year back, time that there old dovecot wor built. Maybe it run dry, and another wor made where you gets your water now."   He jerked a thumb towards the cottage and its pump by the back door.

"Seems likely," Frank agreed.

"Ah.   But them old folks ought to 'ave fill 'er up instead o' puttin' boards across an' coverin' 'em with earth.   Might 'a' known they'd rot.   I near as no matter bruck my neck!"

Brian meanwhile was peering down the hole.   At the bottom he could see the fallen fragments of wood and grass-tufts which had covered it from sight.   Its depth seemed to be between eighteen and twenty feet, though originally this had no doubt been much greater; a glance showed that the sides had collapsed inwards in several places.

"Well, it's lucky no harm was done," Frank replied to Nix's remark.   "When you've finished the wall, perhaps you'd tackle the job of filling this in?"

"Ah, I don' mind.   I could barrer some earth an' rubbidge from over by them brambles an' tip 'em down.   'Ont take more'n couple o' days.   But I can't do it this 'ere week—I've promised to do a job for Mr. Gorringe over at Lease Farm termorrer. Maybe come nex' Monday or Toosday I'll set about that there," Nix added as he started to right the over-turned barrow and carry on with his wall-building.

"If we had another barrow we could make a start on it ourselves," suggested Brian.

"Oh no," replied Frank decisively.   "You're here on holiday, and so am I if it comes to that.   And anyway it's not urgent."

The two turned back towards the house, taking a path that led past the dovecot. As Frank came opposite the door he paused. "You were asking about this old place yesterday," he said. "Like to have a look inside?"

He gave a push to the heavy door, which opened with a protesting creak of massive and rusty hinges. Brian followed him in. The stone-floored lower chamber was dim, but by the light coming through the open doorway Brian saw that it was now used as a storeroom for garden tools and a good deal of miscellaneous junk. A ladder led upwards to the floor above.

Following his host, he ascended. There was more light here, coming through the apertures where the pigeons had once gone in and out. Sunk in the thickness of the walls were rows of cavities, each with a right-angle bend in it, intended as nesting-boxes for the birds. The whole place was deep in dust and litter; though the pigeons had long since vanished, sparrows and starlings had taken possession of the deserted building.

Descending again, Frank and Brian returned towards the house. As they entered by the back door, Brian saw a stout countrywoman sitting on the chair that Nix had recently occupied, busy changing her shoes. Mrs. Pratley had arrived.

"That's a lot easier," she remarked with a grin as

she wriggled her feet into a pair of burst carpet-slippers. "You young folk dunno what it is to 'ave corns. Still, there's wuss things what can 'appen— what price that feller what was found dead up the road yesterday?"

"That valet or whatever he was who worked for Mr. Lethwick, you mean? So you've heard about that?"

"Ah. 'Twas the talk o' the village las' night. Mr. Watts the p'liceman do say there'll be a ninquest. That there Romsey, 'e wasn't the sort us folks likes —comes from Birmin'm or somewheres, 'e did. Nosey sort, 'e was. Nigh as bad as 'is boss, what's always pokin' round with a cigar in 'is face an' tellin' us Kinford people what we oughta do, but 'ont stand for anyone tellin' *'im* anythin'! They was two of a kind, and I've 'eard tell as 'ow two of a kind don' agree. An' Romsey found layin' in the road— makes you think, thass what I say!"

Slipping away from Mrs. Pratley's voluble tongue, and leaving her to think up further libellous hints, Frank and Brian passed on to the sitting-room. Here they found Pamela, who wanted to know what Nix had been fussing about, and, when told, insisted on going out to have a look at the discovery.

When she returned she found them both idling by the fire, and demanded to know what they were going to do with themselves.

"Hadn't thought about it," admitted Frank.

"Why not take Brian for a run round and see something of the neighbourhood?" suggested Pamela promptly.

"Why yes, that's an idea," her brother agreed. "We could go off after lunch and have tea out somewhere. That suit you?" he added to Brian.

As soon as lunch was over, Frank got out his car from where it stood in the shed beside Brian's, and a start was made. Pamela had intended to come with them, but had changed her mind. "I'll give you a list of the shopping I want done," she had said, "and you can get the things in whatever town you decide to stop for your tea."

They drove down to the village. On reaching it Frank turned in the direction opposite to that from which Brian had come on the previous day. They passed the small but ancient church. "Vicarage," said Frank, nodding towards a dismal-looking house beside it. "The vicar's a queer old stick of the name of Quaintance. Hardly ever goes out. Spends all his time, I'm told, poring over abstruse theological books."

Three-quarters of a mile from the village they went by the drive gate of the Manor, and Brian, remembering what Frank had said about his cottage and the old dovecot once belonging to that estate, asked about its present owner.

"I've met him once or twice," replied Frank. "He's a chap about forty, I should say—rather the red-faced sporting and fox-hunting type to look at, if you know what I mean. Goes in for breeding pedigree cattle on a large scale and is rather well known in that line—you can see those up-to-date cowsheds of his yonder." Frank pointed through a gap in the roadside trees, where a number of roofs were visible behind the big house and its garden.

"Married, and with a family, I suppose?" said Brian.

"No, Goodman's a bachelor, and the house is run by a married couple who act as cook and butler. There's a girl of about Pamela's age living there too —Goodman's niece, I understand. I've seen her about the village."

They drove on steadily along the winding roads, climbing the bare wolds and descending into wooded valleys. Turning west, they reached the crest of the sharp drop into the Vale of Evesham, and at the foot of the steep hill turned into a main road that ran parallel with the base of the escarpment. "You wouldn't think," commented Frank presently, point-ing upwards, "that here we're not much more than a mile from where we started. We've been circling round, and Kinford is only a little way beyond that brow above us.   Climb through that wood and over the crest, and you're there!"

Continuing along the road they reached a small town.   Frank parked the car, and the two started off on foot to do Pamela's shopping.   When they had returned to dump the parcels Frank nodded towards a tea-shop in the narrow main street.   "They give you quite a decent tea there, so we'll go across and have some."

They entered the place and sat down at one of the tables.   A rather languid young woman, obviously trying to ape a popular film-star, drifted up.   She faded off again, swinging her hips in what she imagined was the Hollywood fashion, and at length reappeared with what had been ordered.

The restaurant was by no means empty, for about half-a-dozen of the other tables were occupied. Brian glanced round casually before setting to work on the tea and crumpets.   He made a few remarks, and then realised that Frank's attention was occupied elsewhere.   His interest was concentrated on a couple of men who sat at an adjacent table.

Brian wondered why.   There seemed nothing very outstanding about them except that they were an oddly assorted pair.   One was an elderly and dried-up type of individual, with a colourless face and a beaky nose, who might have been a lawyer or bank manager or something of that sort from his

3

clothes and general appearance. The other was younger and of a far rougher type, with restless eyes and hair that wanted cutting. One lock hung over his forehead, which he continually pushed back only to have it fall forward again.

Frank seemed to be trying to listen-in to what they were saying. Brian reflected that he could not be hearing much, for they were speaking low and only a word here and there was audible. He caught Frank's eye and raised his brows questioningly. The other gave a very slight shake to his head and helped himself to some more tea. He ceased to show any obvious interest in the two men beyond an occasional swift glance in their direction.

About ten minutes later the older and more opulent man got up, collected his hat and lighted a cigar. The film-star's understudy, otherwise the waitress, detached herself from the wall against which she had been leaning. Brian guessed that the fat tip she had been expecting did not materialise, for she cast a withering look at the man's back as he passed out into the street.

Presently the other fellow rose, paid up, and moved towards the door. His eyes rested on Frank for a moment, and though he gave no sign of having recognised him, Brian felt certain that he had done so.

As soon as the man had left the shop, Frank was

on his feet. "Pay for us both, and join me where we parked the car," he said hurriedly, and the next instant he, too, was out in the street.

Wondering what was up, Brian squared the account and followed. Frank was nowhere in sight, so following his instructions, Brian strolled in the direction of where they had left the car.

He took his seat in it and waited. Nearly a quarter of an hour elapsed before Frank reappeared.

"What's all the fun and games?" asked Brian. "That chap you were chasing a friend of yours or something?"

"Tell you later," said Frank shortly. "Let's get out of here. We'll take a different, and quicker, road home." He pressed the starter and turned the car.

They drove in silence till they were clear of the little town and running along the base of the high ground towards where the nearest road branched off to climb the steep ascent.

Presently Frank drew in to the side of the road and stopped the car.

"Look here, Brian," he began. "When you first arrived I saw that you were all agog to know what I have been doing recently and the reason why I vanished into silence and never answered those letters of yours. Being a police matter and rather 'top secret', I had no intention of telling you. But what has happened this afternoon makes me think I had better do so—in fact as things are you may become involved during your stay with me and Pamela —though of course you understand what I say goes no further."

Brian nodded. "Of course. I'll keep my mouth shut. Carry on."

"Right. Then this is the way of it. To go back to the beginning, I was always keen on the detective side of police work, and after the usual basic training I got myself attached to that branch. Now, as you must have seen in the papers, there have been a number of extremely well-planned robberies of mail in recent times, especially of consignments of notes sent between the big banks by registered post. Occasionally one or two of the actual thieves have been caught, but they were small fry carrying out orders and knowing nothing of who was organising the whole set-up."

"You mean there was some 'king of crime', as the detective stories have it, in the background?" said Brian.

Frank shrugged. "You can put it that way if you like, though it's an extravagant expression. Anyway, there was never a ghost of a clue as to who had planned these affairs to the last detail—could be anyone from a peer to a parson, and almost certainly someone leading an outwardly blameless life. As a result I was one of those asked to volunteer for undercover work, which meant disappearing into what is known as the underworld, and through his contacts trying to get a line on the fellow. It involved an entire change of identity and the severing of all connexion with my previous existence. It entailed taking on some menial job and, acting the part of a young fellow with criminal leanings, keeping my eyes and ears open."

Brian nodded. He understood now the reason for the look of strain he had noticed on Frank's face, the result of having to be always on his guard and never letting slip any hint as to who he really was.

"Months lengthened into years," Frank went on, "without any real result. True, I got wise to one or two of those who passed on his plans to the actual thieves, but there was never a clue to the man from whom they received those orders. Then something I said or did must have aroused suspicion. I was coshed one night and left insensible in the street. I was picked up by a bobby on the beat and recovered in hospital; but, of course, being spotted, my usefulness in that line was over. I was given this present long leave before returning to routine duties."

"You seem to have had a thin time," commented Brian. "What now?" he went on. "Where does

this little by-play in the tea-shop this afternoon con-
nect up with it?"

"I told you just now that I'd located one or two
of those who passed on the orders to the men who
carried them out. The lieutenants of the unknown
boss, in fact," replied Frank. "Well, that rather
rough-looking bloke who went out of the tea-shop
last was one of them."

"The deuce he was! I shouldn't have thought a
little town like the one we've just left offered much
scope for that sort of thing."

"None at all, I should say," answered Frank.
"Yet it was definitely Budgeon—I'd know his ugly
mug anywhere."

"He spotted you too."

"I'm aware of it. It must have given him a shock,
for he has no doubt reckoned I've been effectually
put out of the way. What's Budgeon doing in these
parts?—that's what I want to know. It's right off
his usual beat."

"Perhaps he's here on holiday."

Frank dismissed the idea with a shrug.

"There was another man at the same table," Brian
went on. "Any notion who *he* was?"

"That's almost the queerest part of it," replied
Frank. "That was Lethwick."

"What? The man who lives in that glaring new

house at Kinford, the employer of the fellow I found in the road?"

"That's the chap.   Now what was he doing in that tea-shop, and how is it that he knows Budgeon?"

"May have gone in for a cup after seeing an undertaker or someone about funeral arrangements for his man Romsey, and by chance sat down at the same table with the other," suggested Brian.   "I understand Lethwick likes chatting with anyone he happens to meet."

"Yes, that's so," Frank admitted.   "It's one of the things that annoys the villagers.   Too chatty and interfering by half.   All the same, it's rum."

"In what way?"   Brian paused, and then added with a grin, "Got the idea that your Budgeon friend was reporting to his unknown boss, and that you've at last got a clue to the man you've been trying to locate for years?"

Frank shrugged.   "It's not impossible.   An obscure tea-shop might be just the sort of place that would be chosen by anyone intent on remaining anonymous and not letting even his lieutenants know where he lived."

"Well, going to do anything about it?"

"Dunno.   Must think it over," replied Frank as he restarted the car and changed gear to take the steep hill that led up to the main Cotswold plateau.

CHAPTER III

INQUEST

"HULLO, you're back earlier than I expected," said Pamela as her brother and Brian returned to the cottage. "Had a good time? Did you get the things I wanted?"

Frank's only reply was a grunt of assent as he dumped the parcels on the table.

The girl glanced sharply at him. "What's up? You and Brian haven't had a bust-up or something?" she asked bluntly.

Brian laughed, while Frank shook his head and smiled. "Heavens no!" he replied. "Sorry I seemed a bit grumpy—I was thinking. As a matter of fact I had rather an unexpected encounter when we were having tea."

"You'd better tell me about it right away, and get it off your chest!"

"All right, I will." Frank dropped into a chair beside where Brian had already seated himself. Pamela remained standing, her hands on her hips, while he told her of the meeting in the tea-shop and the speculations it had raised.

"So you think this man, Budgeon you call him, had come to these parts to collect orders?" the girl asked.

"Could be. From what I know of him, he never does anything without some good reason. Bad reason, rather."

"Did you see which way he went after he left the shop?"

"I followed for some distance and lost him up a side street. He was walking fast and seemed in a hurry."

"And he seemed on friendly terms with Mr. Lethwick?"

"So it appeared. Mind you, as Brian said, it might have been just chance they were at the same table, and Lethwick likes laying down the law to anyone he meets. Anyway, something was being earnestly discussed, though I couldn't hear what. It all seemed a bit odd for just a coincidence."

"And Mr. Lethwick's already in the limelight, so to speak, over his man Romsey being found in the road yesterday?" said Pamela with a smile.

Frank laughed. "You've been listening to Mrs. P! I can't see that's in any way connected with what we saw this afternoon."

The girl shrugged. "Probably not, though you must admit that three odd things have happened during the last twenty-four hours. That was one of them; the second was the discovery of the old well which Nix nearly fell into; and the third is what you've just told me. To quote Mrs. Pratley: 'it makes yer think!' "

"Oh, that's absurd," said Frank, though without real conviction. It was more that he disliked having his vague thoughts put into words by his young sister.

"I expect it is. All the same, what are you going to do about seeing your friend Budgeon in these parts?" went on Pamela remorselessly. "Going to report it?"

"And probably get snubbed for my pains!" retorted Frank. "Still, I don't know—perhaps I ought," he went on after a pause. "I might put a call through to Copthorne in London—he's a detective inspector and was my superior officer when I was on the job. He's a reasonable chap, and wouldn't get shirty even though he thought there was nothing in it."

Frank rose to his feet and went over to the side-table where the telephone instrument stood. He lifted the receiver and asked for a London number.

It took some time to get through to the man he wanted. When contact was at last made, he described the afternoon's encounter.

"We happen to be aware," came the voice from the other end, "that Budgeon's on holiday from the place he works. Oh yes, knowing what we do about him, we keep tabs on him and hear fast enough if he's not in his usual haunts. Taking a holiday might account for his being in your area. Or it might not. Who was the man you saw him talking with?"

Frank told what he knew of Lethwick, which was little enough, and almost apologetically added the idea he had formed that Lethwick might be the man they had long been seeking.

"I wouldn't say it's impossible," said Inspector Copthorne guardedly. "You say he's a comparative newcomer to your village? I'll have enquiries made about where he came from and what he's been doing in the past. In the meantime keep an eye lifting, and if there are any more developments, or if you see Budgeon again, give me a ring. I could come down myself if necessary, but there's no point in going into that yet. G'bye!"

Frank put down the receiver and turned to tell those who waited what the inspector had said.

Brian had hardly got down next morning when he saw the uniformed figure of P.C. Watts approaching the front door. "He's after you, I expect," said Frank with a grin. "You'd better go and see what he wants."

Brian did so. "Mornin', sir," said the constable.

"Summons to attend the inquest on James Romsey
—the chap me an' you found in the road. Two-
thirty 'safternoon, in the big room back o' the
'Rising Sun'."

"Right, I'll be there."

"Ah. An' don' you forget. Two-thirty sharp,
that is if Mr. Spencer the coroner turn up in time."
Having handed over the order, the village bobby
took himself off.

"I'll come along down with you," announced
Frank later at lunch. "The weather's cleared," he
added, referring to the rain that had fallen earlier
in the day, "so we might as well walk. Hardly
worth while getting out a car for that short distance."

They reached the inn a few minutes before the
appointed time, to find quite a number of people,
mainly women, grouped round the door at the back.
Entertainments were rare in Kinford, and this had
the added merit of being free.

Frank nodded to one or two whom he knew. "I
don't see Lethwick," he commented in a low voice
to Brian, "but I expect he's inside. He'll have to
be here as Romsey's employer. I suppose we'd
better go along in too."

As he spoke a large car drew up and a red-faced
man in tweeds got out. Brian thought that this was
probably the coroner, but Frank's remark, "Hullo,
here's Goodman," told him that the new arrival was

the owner of the Manor. The description Frank
had given of him was apt, but Brian put him down
as older than Frank's estimate—fifty was nearer the
mark than forty.

"Ha, Tilney!" said Goodman as he approached.
"Thought I'd better come down and see what was
doing. Magistrate and all that, hmm!" He glanced
at Brian and added, "It was your friend here found
him, wasn't it?"

Frank introduced Brian, who said that he had.

"Must ha' given you a shock. Coroner not turned
up yet?" Goodman went on, glancing towards the
open door where P.C. Watts had taken up his stand.

"Not as far as we know."

"Huh! Spencer's no slave to the clock—never
was. Poring over some conveyance in his office and
forgotten the time, most likely. By the way, Tilney,
what's this yarn going round the village about the
discovery of an old well in your orchard?"

Frank told him.

"Interesting," said Goodman. "I'd like to see it.
Anything down there, I wonder? I've quite a collection of things that have been dug up in the
neighbourhood. You ought to come up to the
Manor and have a look at them. Prehistoric stuff
mostly—Stone Age and all that."

"Thanks, though I doubt if there's anything of
that kind down the old well. It's half filled in with

fallen rubbish. But come and inspect it any time you like."

"What about to-day? You walked down here, eh?" replied Goodman. "I'll run you both back in my car when this affair is over, and see it then. Ah, here's Spencer at last!" he added as another car drew up. "Only ten minutes late!"

There was a concerted move into the building. The coroner took his seat, and after the usual preliminaries the inquest began.

Lethwick was called first to confirm the identity of Romsey. Heads turned as he rose from where he was sitting. He answered the questions put to him with deliberation and in a somewhat harsh voice. Brian had a good view of the man's profile, with its dried-up colourless skin and jutting nose, and he wondered whether he was indeed the master criminal that Frank seemed to think. He might very well be so, but he realised it was one thing to suspect, and quite another to produce any shred of proof.

Brian, as the finder of the body, was called next to make his statement, and Watts the policeman followed to describe how he had been fetched and what he had done. All this was just routine; it was the medical evidence that was the important part of the proceedings.

The doctor described Romsey's injuries, which

apparently were numerous and ranged from a broken skull to several cracked ribs.

"Do you consider," asked the coroner presently in his dry legal voice, "that the results of your examination are consistent with the supposition that the man Romsey was struck by a moving vehicle?"

"They might be—I won't go further than that," retorted the doctor. "They might equally well have been caused by other means."

Remembering Mrs. Pratley's libellous remark, Brian glanced sideways at Frank, and caught his eye turned in his own direction.

The coroner seemed somewhat taken aback—he had expected a more definite answer. He brought up the question of the marks of muddy tyres seen on the man's clothing, but the doctor refused to budge from his original statement. He agreed that the man had probably been run over, but that was as far as he would go, and the coroner had to be content with that. In the end the verdict of manslaughter by motor vehicle against some person or persons unknown was given, which left it to the police to find out, if they could, who had been driving recklessly along that winding country lane.

To a shuffling of feet and a murmur of talk the room began to empty. "I'd just as soon walk back," Frank remarked to Brian as they emerged into the open, "but as Goodman has offered us a lift we'd better wait by his car till he comes along."

Goodman appeared a couple of minutes later, having waited to have a few words with the coroner. The three got in, and its owner turned the big car into the road leading up the slad.

The cottage was reached. Frank introduced the visitor to Pamela who though she had seen him about the village, had not so far met him. After a few minutes' general conversation a move was made to the orchard and the gaping hole that Nix's heavy barrow had revealed.

Goodman peered down the old well and made several comments about it, though Brian had the impression that he was not really very interested in it after all. Goodman had said that his line was Stone Age curiosities, so presumably this relic of medieval days was too recent in date to rouse his enthusiasm.

As they turned away and began to retrace their steps towards the house, Goodman made some reference to the inquest they had just attended.

"That doctor didn't seem at all certain that the fellow met his end from a road accident," put in Brian.

"Huh! That's nothing," said Goodman with a shrug. "Doctors are always cautious beggars and scared of making definite statements. Somebody ran him down, and that's all there is to it. Feller's no great loss to Kinford—no more liked in the village than Lethwick is!"

This seemed a good opportunity to Frank to find out more about Lethwick. Goodman was an old resident, and would know as much as anyone in the locality.

"Never taken to the feller!" said Goodman in his downright way in reply to Frank's question. "Came here two or three years ago, or maybe four, and built that shocking house of his. Talks a lot and gets on the wrong side of the villagers, and yet never gives away any information about himself. Supposed to be retired from business. What sort o' business? Shouldn't be surprised if there were something fishy about him."

"The same idea occurred to me," said Frank.

"Did it? Then maybe you're not far wrong. Well, I must get along back. Come up to the Manor one day, both of you, and have a look at my collection of neolithic finds. Bring your sister, too, Tilney—she'd be company for my niece Sybil. She seldom sees any girls of her own age—there don't seem to be any around these parts nowadays."

The visitor drove away, and Frank and Brian turned again towards the house. "Decent sort, Goodman," commented the former.

4

"Yes, I thought so too. He spoke of the niece. What's she like?"

"Dunno. Only seen her in the distance, but she might be worth knowing. I say, Pamela," Frank went on as they rejoined the girl indoors, "we've just received an invitation to go up to the Manor and inspect Goodman's bits o' rubbish that he collects as a hobby, and you're to come with us and make yourself pleasant to that niece of his, my girl!"

"Perhaps she'd appreciate *you* making yourself pleasant to her more than me!" retorted Pamela. "I'm not the sort to go in for girlish confidences and all that sort of bunk! When's this excitement to come off?"

"Oh, nothing fixed—open invitation to go when we like."

"That's a relief—I thought you'd gone and committed me to a definite date. And now I want to hear about the inquest; was it brought in as an accident, or is Mrs. Pratley going to get the thrill of her life by declaring that she'd 'said so all along'?"

CHAPTER IV

CHASE IN THE NIGHT

A COLD fog blanketed the wolds next morning, and for those at Slad Cottage it increased the attractions of the warm fire in the sitting-room. By the middle of the afternoon however the atmosphere became clearer, and Brian, feeling he needed some exercise, announced that he was going for a stroll.

"If that's so, you can go down to the village shop and get me one or two oddments I know are stocked there," said Pamela. "Do you know where it is? Well, you can't miss it anyway, for there isn't another. It's nearly opposite the inn."

"Right, I'll get them for you," replied Brian. "Coming, Frank?"

"No, I've a repair job to do on one of the cupboards in the kitchen. Mrs. P. has been complaining for some time about a broken hinge, and I'd better see to it before I forget. You carry on, though."

The mist had gone but the air was cold, and Brian walked briskly along the road down the slad. He turned into the village street, and presently caught

sight of a small window behind which were displayed
sundry tins and soap packets and scrubbing-brushes.
He pushed open the door alongside and entered.

There was only one customer in the shop, a girl.
As Brian came in she was thrusting her purchases
into a bag, and she gave him an almost startled look,
dropping one of her parcels as she did so. Brian
stooped and retrieved it for her. She smiled and
thanked him, but before Brian had had time to take
in more than the facts that she was slim, with
dark hair, and rather smartly dressed, she had moved
to the door and disappeared into the street.

"Good afternoon," said the middle-aged man
behind the counter. "You'll be the gent what's
stoppin' up the slad, I make no doubt. And what
can I get for you?"

"Oh, good afternoon," said Brian, bringing back
his thoughts to the business in hand. "Yes, I'm
staying with Mr. Tilney." He handed over the list
that Pamela had given him, and added, "Who was
the girl that's just gone out? I'm afraid I startled
her when I came in."

"That's the young lady what lives at the Manor
—Mr. Goodman's niece. She do be a bit shy, like,
but then she hardly see nobody up at that big house,
for Mr. Goodman don't entertain, him not bein'
married."

"Oh, so that's Miss Goodman. I wondered who she was."

"Miss Kelly's her name, Miss Sybil Kelly," corrected the proprietor. "She's the daughter of the lady what was Mr. Goodman's sister, a widow what died a couple o' years back. It was then Miss Kelly come to Kinford permanent, like. Took her in to live, seein' she'd nowhere to go, Mr. Goodman did."

"Decent of him," commented Brian, for something to say.

"Ah." The shopkeeper was quite ready to talk. He placed his hands on the counter, on either side of the goods from Pamela's list. "Mr. Goodman's always been very well liked in the village. And them as he employs with them pedigree cattle up at the Manor never had no complaint against him, not like some I could mention. But goin' back to the young lady, it's a shame she don't see more young people. Time she first came she was different somehow, but recent she's changed and looks nervous and worried. Comes o' livin' with nobody of her own age and kind to make friends with, I reckon."

"Yes, I can understand that. I know Miss Tilney is going along soon to make her acquaintance."

"Ah, that 'ud be a real kindness." The owner of the shop lifted his hands from the counter and began to extract Brian's change from the till. As he did so a new figure entered, preceded by a gust of cigar-smoke.   Brian recognised him instantly.

Lethwick strode up to the counter and demanded to know why something that he had ordered had not been sent.   "No wonder you village shopkeepers never make money," he went on.   "Why don't ya run ya business on business lines and keep an assistant and a delivery-van, hey?"

"One moment, sir—I'm just giving this gentleman his change."   The tone was cold, and bore out what Brian had heard about the opinion of the village as regards Lethwick.

Thus momentarily checked, Lethwick turned his eyes towards Brian.   "Seen ya before," he announced. "At the inquest yesterday, and before that, too." He mentioned the restaurant in which Brian and Frank had encountered him, and added with a snort, "Plenty o' room in the place, but I'd hardly sat down when a common sort o' feller plumped himself opposite me an' started talking as if he'd known me all my life.   That sort has plenty o' cheek!   I gave him some good advice.   Don't suppose he'll take it, though—I know a waster when I see one.   What ya doin' in Kinford, hey?   Havin' ya holiday?   You young chaps get nothing but holidays!"   Lethwick turned again to the proprietor.   "Now then, what about those things o' mine?"

Brian picked up his change and passed out into

the street where the dusk of the winter day was already gathering. There was a thoughtful look on his face.

" 'Makes you think', as Mrs. Pratley says," he murmured to himself. "Why, as soon as he saw me, should Lethwick bring up the subject of his companion at the tea-shop and insist that he'd never met him before, in spite of the way they seemed to be talking so earnestly? It *might* be so, but in that case, why stress it? Presumably to bluff me into believing it was a chance encounter and not pre-arranged. Obviously he hopes I'll report what he said to Frank, which means he must be aware that Frank knows who Budgeon is, and wants to stop any possible suspicions. As far as I'm concerned, it had the opposite effect!"

With his purchases under his arm Brian turned off the village street and along the road up the slad. Darkness was coming on rapidly, and far ahead of him the yellow gleam of a lighted window marked his destination.

He had covered nearly half the distance when, a little way in front and to his left, he heard a creak of wood and the scrape of a boot. A moment later he made out the form of a figure climbing a road-side gate. Brian had been walking on the grass verge, and the man had not heard his approach.

The fellow dropped into a field beyond the gate

and paused to light a cigarette before going on. As he struck a match he heard the sound of steps on the soft grass. Instantly he blew out the flame and remained motionless. But in the momentary gleam Brian had caught a glimpse of his face. It seemed vaguely familiar.

Brian had not gone on more than twenty yards when with a start he realised where he had previously seen that hatless face with its dangling lock of hair. If it were not Budgeon, the companion of Lethwick in the tea-shop, it was his exact double.

Brian halted. It occurred to him he would look a prize fool if he gave chase to some farmworker returning home across the fields; while even if the man were Budgeon he did not see what he could do about it. An evening stroll is no crime, nor is climbing a gate unless damage is done. He could only carry on, and report what he had seen to Frank.

Brian got back, and gave his friend an account of what had taken place since going down to the village. "Queer about Lethwick," commented Frank. "If he's the clever chap we take him for, why did he over-play his hand by saying what he did to you? He can wait, however; what's more urgent is this fellow you saw on the way back. Which way did he appear to be going?"

Brian told him.

"Now why? Nothing but fields, and so on, in

that direction as far as I know. I'm off to have a scout round. Even if it isn't the man you think there will be no harm done. Coming?

Before Brian could answer, Pamela put in a word. "It's dark now—you won't be able to see your way, much less find anybody. Don't be an ass, Frank. After all, you're on holiday, and not here to chase round after suspected crooks. Be sensible and chuck the idea."

"Not much!" Frank retorted. "It isn't pitch dark anyway, for there's a young crescent moon that won't be setting for nearly a couple of hours. Besides, we'll take torches. Possibly it's a wasted effort, but I'm used to that in my job. I don't expect we'll be out long."

"Keep on the verge and don't talk," said Frank as they hastened along the dark road.

Brian indicated the gate, and they climbed over. It was useless to look for spoor on the grass, even had the ground not been hardening with the frost that was following the cold day. However, a thin line of shorter turf indicated a little-used footpath, and Frank followed it, as it seemed the most likely route.

The two crossed a sloping field. A loose-stone wall and a gate barred their way. On the farther side they found themselves on much wilder ground, dotted with gorse bushes and patches of withered bracken and dead willow-herb. The faint track had disappeared. Both instinctively slowed their pace, so as not to make too much noise against the scrubby vegetation.

For some minutes they moved onwards, with Brian feeling that the whole thing was rather a waste of time and energy. There was no knowing which way the fellow had gone, and he wanted his tea. Still, he felt he must back up Frank and not be the first to suggest chucking it and going home.

A slight noise made them both halt and peer into the gloom. Someone was moving across their front —they could hear the rustle of dry bracken against his legs. The sound ceased, and there was the glimmer of a torch quickly switched on and off. Whoever held it seemed to be kneeling over something on the ground.

Frank made a gesture to his companion and the two moved forward as silently as possible. But the crouching man heard them; he sprang to his feet and made off at a shambling run.

Brian and Frank promptly gave chase. They were young and active, and gained rapidly on the dark figure in front. The fugitive seemed to realise that he had no hope of getting away, for after bending as if to thrust something under a gorse bush, he straightened himself and turned to face his pursuers.

Frank flashed on his torch, revealing the weathered and unshaven features of—Nix!

The surprise of the hunters was only equalled by that of the hunted. "Whoy, if it ent Mr. Tilney an' 'is friend!" exclaimed Nix when he discovered who they were. "I reckoned for sure it wor that there Watts arter me."

"Meaning that you were doing a spot of poaching?" grinned Frank.

"I wouldn't go for to call it that," replied Nix in a huffy tone. "What's the 'arm in settin' a few snares? Nobody don' bother about the shootin' on these 'ere rough wolds, so why shouldn't I get summat for me dinner now an' agen?"

"No reason as far as I'm concerned!" laughed Frank. "We weren't looking for you, we were after someone else. Seen anybody round this way the last half-hour or so?"

"Ah, it's a rum-'un you should ask that, mister. I did see a bloke making across over yonder. Looked as 'ow 'e was goin' to pass along back o' that orchard o' yours. Made me wonder what 'e was a-doin' on. There ent nothin' out beyond that way to take anybody this time o' night."

"Thanks for the tip," said Frank. "We'll push on in the direction you say he went. Sorry to have given you a scare, Nix. Don't forget," he added as he and Brian turned away, "to retrieve those snares you shoved under that gorse!"

Nix gave an answering grin. "So you see me push 'em there? Wasn't no sense in lettin' Watts find 'em on me, an' it was 'im I reckoned you was. Seein' as 'ow it ent, back they goes in me pocket!"

The two pushed on between the gorse bushes and clumps of dead bracken. Stumbles were frequent, for the sinking crescent of the moon gave little light, and to use their torches might warn the man they were trying to trail that he was being followed. Another stone wall intervened, with more open wold beyond it, where the sheep-bitten turf made progress far easier. Brian guessed that somewhere to their right lay Slad Cottage, while to their left he could just make out the dark blur of the woods that crowned the sharp descent to the low-lying country to the west.

There was no sign of anyone moving in front.

Presently Frank halted. "It's no go!" he remarked. "There's nothing to tell us where that chap went. Anyhow, very possibly you were mistaken and it wasn't Budgeon after all. I don't suppose Nix is the only fellow out poaching round these parts to-night."

"Nix saw him, and he would have known if he were a local man," Brian objected.

"That proves nothing. I expect poachers from

a distance aren't above invading ground over which others of their kind think they have a proprietary right!" Frank replied with a laugh. "We're wasting our time. Let's be getting back."

They turned down the slope in the direction of Slad Cottage, approaching it from the rear. They reached the wall surrounding the orchard, clambered over it, and dropped on the other side. The old dovecot loomed up before them, a thick black finger rising against the night sky. Frank led the way round it, and took the path that ran towards the back door of the cottage.

"Mind the hole!" Brian called out.

"I haven't forgotten it." Frank reached the place and paused. "It was too dim there to see anything when we looked down by daylight, but by shining a torch into it now it might be easier to see more clearly what it's like." He knelt on the edge, aimed his powerful torch downwards, and pushed over the switch.

There was a flash, and the thing went dead.

"Bulb blown, confound it!" grunted Frank. "Lend me yours, will you?" He laid his own on the ground beside him and took the one that Brian handed him.

The downward-directed rays revealed nothing of fresh interest, only the broken-sided shaft half filled with fallen rubbish. Frank rose again to his feet, and the two continued on their way to the cottage.

As they reached the back door Frank gave an exclamation of annoyance.

"Blowed if I didn't put down that dud torch of mine and never picked it up again! This one's yours." Frank handed the one he carried to Brian. "I'd better slip back and fetch it, or it'll be all rusty by morning. You carry on and get started with your tea."

He turned to retrace his steps by the light of the sinking crescent of moon, while Brian entered the house.

"So here you are at last," said Pamela as he appeared. "Did you find the man you were looking for?"

Brian shook his head. "There was nothing to tell us which way he had gone. The only person we struck was Nix—doing a bit of poaching."

"He amuses himself that way most nights, I believe. Where's Frank?" the girl added as she poured out Brian's tea.

"He's gone back to fetch his torch." Brian explained about their halt on the way home at the old well. "I don't suppose he'll be long."

It was not until more than ten minutes had passed, and Brian had finished his second cup, that

it struck him Frank was taking his time. "I wonder
what he's up to?" he remarked.

"Delayed by something, I suppose." Pamela rose
and refilled the teapot from the kettle simmering on
the hearth. "This won't be drinkable if he doesn't
come soon."

Still Frank did not reappear. "I'm going to look
for him," said Brian, getting to his feet.

"I'll come too," said Pamela, catching the note of
anxiety in his voice. "Wait a moment while I find
another torch. Oh, here it is."

Together they went out. The moon had just set
and it was now pitch dark. Shining the lights in
front of their feet, they started along the path towards the dovecot.

CHAPTER V

THE UNCOVERED WELL

BRIAN shouted, expecting to hear Frank's reply from somewhere out in the darkness, but he received no answer. He and Pamela reached the spot where Frank had left his torch. It no longer lay beside the old well-shaft, nor was there any sign of its owner. Calling again, the two swung the beams of their own torches over the surrounding grass and shrubs.

Half-a-dozen yards away Brian's eye caught a gleam of reflected light. Keeping his own rays on the spot, he strode towards it. The thing which glinted was Frank's missing torch, lying with its glass broken where it had apparently been flung.

"It's his all right," said Pamela as her companion handed it to her, "but why should he chuck it away like that? From what you said it only needed a new bulb. And where on earth can Frank have gone?"

"Ask me another. Perhaps he's remembered something he wanted to fetch from the dovecot." They crossed over to it, but the place was empty.

Emerging, they shouted once more, their combined voices loud enough to be heard half a mile away. The only result was the startled chirping of some roosting birds.

"Queer! Where the deuce can he have gone?"

Peering this way and that, they retraced their steps towards the old well. "He can't have slipped in *there*, by any chance—he knew all about it," murmured Brian, half to himself. He stepped forward and flashed his torch down the shaft.

Lying on the rubbish at the bottom was Frank's huddled and motionless figure.

Both gave exclamations of dismay. The girl knelt on the brink, but Brian promptly pulled her back. "Edge may be rotten," he said shortly. "Got a rope anywhere?"

"I believe there's one in the dovecot."

Brian ran to fetch it. He discovered it lying under some junk and hauled it out. "Hope to goodness it's long enough," he muttered to himself as he hurried back. "I'll have to hitch one end to something, for Pamela'll never be able to hold my weight while I get down."

The trunk of a nearby apple tree provided an anchor, and the other end proved just sufficiently long to reach the bottom of the hole. Hoping that the rope was reasonably sound and would not break, Brian lowered himself hand over hand.

5

He bent over Frank and gave a sigh of relief when he realised that his friend was not dead. He was bleeding from a gashed head, probably caused by hitting the stone lining as he fell, which had knocked him unconscious, and one arm was doubled under him and most certainly appeared to be broken. Brian saw there was only one thing to do. He must tie the rope round Frank, clamber out himself, and then try to haul him up to the surface.

In the meantime Pamela, who was anxiously waiting at the top, was startled to hear approaching footsteps. She jerked the rays of her torch in the direction of the sound, and saw the figure of Nix coming towards her.

"What's up, miss?" he asked. He jerked a thumb over his shoulder and added, "I was out yonder and I 'ears some-'un 'ollerin' fit to bust, so I comes along."

"Oh, I'm so glad you did! It was us calling—me and Mr. Carter. We've just found my brother down this horrible old well, and——"

There was no need to explain further, for Nix had already seen the rope and heard Brian calling up to Pamela about what he intended to do. He thrust his head over the brink. "Oy, mister!"

Brian jumped. Then recognising the voice, he called back, "Is that you, Nix?"

"Ah. Don' you go for to come up—you stop

where you is and steady 'im time I pulls, so as 'e don'
bump agen them sides. Ready?"

"Yes."

" 'Ere goes, then." Half a minute later Frank
was safely at the top and, with Pamela's help, carefully laid on the ground. Nix untied the rope and
tossed the end down to Brian, who clambered
quickly to the surface.

"An 'urdle's what we wants to carry 'im on, but
there ent none 'ere," commented Nix. "Good job
it ent far. You take one end on 'im, mister, an' I'll
take t'other."

Together Brian and Nix bore Frank back to the
cottage, while Pamela ran on ahead to telephone to
the nearest doctor, five miles away.

Once more inside the cottage they were able to
examine Frank's injuries more thoroughly than had
been possible outside in the darkness. His right
arm was clearly broken, but the bleeding from the
head appeared to come from a bad scrape rather
than a deep wound, though it had been enough to
knock him senseless. The arm would have to be
left to professional skill; but while waiting for the
doctor Pamela and Brian cleaned the dirt and stone-
dust from the other injury and applied a temporary
bandage.

They had hardly finished when Frank gave signs
of returning consciousness. He opened his eyes,

muttered something, and tried to sit up.   Gently
Brian restrained him.

"Take it easy," he said.   "You've had a bit of an
accident."

Frank made another movement, and groaned.
"My arm!"

"Yes, I know.   It's broken, and you got a bang
on the head as well when you tumbled into that well
which Nix found.   A doctor's on his way here now,
and he'll soon make you feel more comfortable."

"I'm beginning to remember—I went back for
that torch——"

"That's right, and you slipped and fell in.   Edge
rotten, probably.   But you ought not to talk."

"I didn't slip—I was pushed!" said Frank
vehemently.   "As I bent to pick the thing up, somebody gave me a violent push from behind!   I went
over, and that's the last I remember."

"Don't worry about that now," put in Pamela
soothingly.   "Do be quiet and stop exciting yourself."

The words had the opposite effect.   "You don't
believe me, but it was so!   I was pushed in!   That
chap Brian and I were looking for must have——"

At that moment the outer door opened and the
doctor bustled in.   Brian saw that he was the same
man who had given evidence at the inquest on
Romsey.

"Now what's all this?" he said briskly and cheer-fully. "Let's have a look at you."

"I——" began Frank.

"Shut up—I'll do the talking that's needed!" Swiftly and competently the doctor made his examination. "Bar bruises and that bump on the head, I don't think there's anything very wrong except that arm," he said presently. "Can't fix that properly here—needs doing in hospital and having it set in plaster. I 'phoned for the local ambulance before I left, so it should be along any time. I think I hear it now," he added, as he caught the hum of a vehicle coming up the slad road.

"I'll come along and look after Frank in the ambulance," said Pamela.

The doctor shook his head. "My dear young lady, you'd much better stop where you are. It's not as if you could do anything, and the instant he gets to hospital we shall be busy with him. In fact you'd be a nuisance, to put it plainly. I'll give you a ring later, and you can come in to-morrow if you like and visit him. We shall probably keep him for a day or two."

As Frank was lifted into the ambulance he beckoned with his sound arm to Brian. "As soon as I'm off," he said, "go back and ring up Inspector Copthorne. Don't forget." He added the number.

"Well, I will if you want me to, but——"

"There's no 'but' about it! Dash it, this is urgent! After what's happened I'm certain you were right, and that chap we followed really was——"

His words were cut short by the driver closing the back of the vehicle. He jumped into his seat, and Brian and Pamela watched the rear-lights grow small in the distance.

They turned to re-enter the cottage. A dark figure was lingering by the door. It was Nix, who had faded off when the doctor arrived.

"Wot's 'e say about 'im?"

"Doesn't think there's anything serious, except that arm," replied Brian.

"Ah. Let us know, mister, 'ow 'e get on. I'll be sayin' good-night now, an' goin' back to what I was doin'."

"Good-night, Nix, and thanks for your help. I'd have had a job to get Mr. Tilney out if you hadn't turned up."

Nix's only reply to that obvious statement was to disappear into the darkness.

Brian and Pamela went back to the sitting-room and sat down almost automatically beside the table with its used cups and the teapot, now cold, that had been refilled for Frank's return. It was Brian who first broke the silence.

"You mustn't worry—he'll be all right. It's lucky

things aren't a lot worse. Thanks to the old well being half choked with rubbish it wasn't very deep."

"I know. But it puzzles me how he came to fall in. Frank knew all about that hole."

"You heard what he said just before the doctor turned up? About being pushed in when he bent to pick up the torch."

The girl nodded. "But he was just recovering from a bad knock on the head and unlikely to re-member things clearly. There was nobody to push him in."

"What about the chap we were chasing, who I am certain was Budgeon. Though we failed to catch up with him, he may very well have seen us, and when we chucked it and started home he may have decided to turn the tables and follow *us*, to see where we came from. Besides, now I come to think of it, there was Frank's dud torch chucked away into the bushes. Frank had no reason to do that, but anyone who pushed him in had. To gain time for his get-away. He would guess we'd presently be coming to look for Frank, and not seeing the torch would reckon he'd picked it up and gone on somewhere. As in fact happened, more or less."

"Yes, I see that," Pamela admitted. "You think the man followed you both into the orchard."

"Yes, and took the opportunity so unexpectedly offered to him of trying to put a stop to Frank's interest in him. The sound of Frank's returning footsteps would have told him Frank was alone," replied Brian. "The existence of that well is common knowledge in the village by now, and no doubt everybody's discussing it. If the man were Budgeon, and if he'd been in touch with Lethwick earlier—though we've no proof on that point—he would probably have been told about it."

Pamela nodded. "It's the second time within a few weeks that Frank's been knocked out," she said in a flat voice.

"Yes, I know, and presumably by the same person or his pals. But we mustn't look back, but forward. With Frank out of action, probably for weeks, with that arm, it's up to me to carry on for him."

Pamela jerked up her head. "Up to us, you mean. I'm not going to sit back and do nothing. I'm in on this as much as you!"

Brian smiled. "Couldn't wish for a better partner!" he said gallantly.

"That's not just words—I mean it. What are we going to do next?"

"Ring up that inspector chap in London. Frank spoke of it as he was being put into the ambulance. Will you do it, or shall I?"

"You'd better," decided Pamela, "considering you've seen this Budgeon person and I haven't, so you can give more details. Tell this Inspector

Copthorne exactly what has happened to Frank, and——"

"All right, all right!" Brian checked the flow, suppressing a grin with difficulty. Why, he wondered, did young women so often say they wanted to leave a thing to you, and then immediately start to tell you exactly what to say and do?

Brian got the number easily enough, but making contact with the man he wanted took some time. Probably, he reflected, Frank had some password which ensured that he should be put through quickly to the right person. At last, however, his efforts met with success.

First he explained who he was, and that he was ringing up for Frank who had been knocked out and taken to hospital. Having identified himself, Brian went on to give an account of the evening's events.

"Sorry to hear about Tilney," came Copthorne's voice over the wire. "From what you say I gather you know a good deal about what he was doing before he went on leave?"

"Yes, he told me about it."

"Hmmm! Shouldn't have done—but no matter. Perhaps it was a good thing as it's turned out, but keep what he told you under your hat."

"Most certainly I will. His sister knows, of course, but that's all. Now about what's happened.

Will you be able to come down?"   Brian added the name of the local hospital where Frank had been taken.

"Better not.   I might be recognised, and if the man we want to get—not Budgeon but his boss—is living in your area, it would put him more than ever on his guard.   At the same time I'd like to question you about details.   Have you got a car?"

"Yes.   Why?"

"Well, Oxford's a convenient centre.   If I run down to-morrow, you could meet me there."

"Certainly I will.   Where do I look for you?   At the main police-station?"

"No.   Too public.   Besides, I shan't be on an official visit, so to speak; we London chaps don't barge in on county constabulary headquarters unless definitely invited."   Copthorne gave the address of a private house in Holywell.   "We'll meet there about 11.30.   Don't drive up—park your car somewhere and walk.   That suit?   G'bye."

"What did he say?" asked Pamela as the receiver was replaced.

Brian told her.

"Did he mention anything about what Frank asked him to find out about Mr. Lethwick?"

"No, but he might not like to on the 'phone, in case somebody at a local exchange was listening in

and got curious. Anyway, I can ask him to-morrow
—he wants me to meet him in Oxford."

"I'll come with you. We can call early at the
hospital to see how Frank is, and carry on from
there."

For a moment Brian wondered whether it would
be wise to take the girl with him. The inspector
had not said anything about wanting to see her too,
and might be annoyed if she turned up. On the
other hand, after what had happened, it might be
as well that she should not remain alone at the cottage. True, Mrs. Pratley would be there, but only
for a limited period, and Brian could not tell how
long he might be away. "Yes certainly—good idea,"
he replied to Pamela's suggestion.

Dinner that evening was a silent meal, for neither
felt much like talking. They had not long finished
when the 'phone rang. "That'll be the doctor!"
exclaimed Pamela as she jumped up to answer it.

Her face showed that the news was good.
"Frank's going on well," she reported as she returned to her seat. "He says there are no complica-
tions or other injuries. His arm's been fixed up
and he's quite comfortable, though of course it'll
have to remain in plaster for some weeks. They're
going to keep him till the day after tomorrow, when
the doctor says we can go along in the car and bring
him home."

CHAPTER VI

APPOINTMENT IN OXFORD

MRS. PRATLEY arrived next morning well before her usual time, all agog for full details about Frank's mishap. Both Brian and Pamela were surprised that she had already heard of it, for it had all happened after dark when most village people are indoors.

"Bless yer, it didn't take us long to know on it!" said Mrs. Pratley with pride. "Mrs. Potter she see the doctor's car turn up the slad, and ten minutes later that there ambulance come along and stop to ask the way off of young Barton what was comin' back late from work. Then down at the pub old Charlie come in for 'is usual pint, and 'e tells 'em all as 'ow 'e'd 'elped to pull Mr. Tilney out o' that there old well."

As she spoke Brian reflected that Scotland Yard had nothing on a village community for finding out things; could use be made of that gift, he wondered, to solve the present problem?

When breakfast was over, Brian went out to start up his car. Pamela joined him and together they drove off, leaving Mrs. Pratley to get on with her usual jobs and to lock up the cottage when she left and park the key in its usual hiding-place.

Halfway down to the village they caught sight of the owner of the Manor, red-faced and clad in hairy tweeds, striding across one of the roadside fields, obviously out for a brisk morning walk. Waving his stick he signalled to them to stop, and Brian did so.

Goodman swung himself over the bordering stone wall and stepped up to the car. "I was on my way over to see you," he said. "What's all this I hear? Is it true your brother had an accident down the old well you showed me a couple of days ago?"

Pamela replied that it was, and that they were now on their way to the hospital to see him.

"Bless my soul, Kinford seems a place for accidents lately!" commented Goodman. "First that feller— what's his name?—Romsey, gets run over, and now your brother's come to grief. Still, lucky it was no worse in his case. Going to see him, eh? Why not come round by the Manor as you return, and let me know how you find him."

"Well, we don't quite know when we'll be back. We have to go on to Oxford afterwards to keep an appointment."

"That so? Well, I mustn't delay you. Remember me to your brother an' all that."

Goodman stepped back, and Brian put the car into gear. He felt slightly annoyed with Pamela for mentioning the Oxford appointment. Not that it mattered in this case with a man like Goodman, and she had not said whom they were meeting, but the inspector had been strong on the point of saying nothing to anyone.

They visited the local hospital and saw Frank, who seemed both cheerful and comfortable. After they had chatted for a short while a nurse came along, and, taking the hint, they brought their visit to a close, promising to call again next day and bring Frank home as arranged.

They continued the journey, and in due course reached the northern fringe of Oxford. "I'd better have a fill up," said Brian as he caught sight of a roadside garage. "Tank's a bit low, and I don't want to stall in traffic."

As he drew in towards the pumps a large black Daimler coming out from Oxford forestalled them. It was not until Brian had drawn up almost alongside to wait his turn that he recognised the driver, who had stepped out and was fumbling in his pocket for cash. It was Lethwick, and a younger man was a passenger in the car.

It was not a meeting Brian wanted, but it was now too late to do anything about it.

Lethwick turned his head and recognised both

Pamela and Brian. "What's all this about Tilney?"
he demanded. "Heard he'd fallen downstairs or
somethin', and been taken to hospital. What ya
doin' here, then?—oughta be sittin' at his bedside,
I should ha' thought."

Brian evaded that last question by saying it was
the old well that had caused Frank's injuries, and
that he was going on favourably.

"That so? Then he's lucky. How did it happen? Bit o' carelessness, I suppose." Lethwick
turned to pay the man at the pump and climbed
back into his driving-seat. He seemed to be in a
hurry to get on.

"Nice sympathetic attitude!" commented Brian
as Lethwick drove away. "I wonder who that chap
was he had in the car. Certainly not Budgeon, but
I shouldn't be surprised if he were another of the
same sort."

"Unless it's his new manservant to replace Romsey," suggested Pamela. "He may have been to
fetch him from the station."

"Why yes, I suppose that's possible, though you'd
have thought he'd have arranged to pick him up
somewhere nearer. It's a long drive in here from
Kinford," replied Brian as he drew in for his fill of
petrol.

Following the instruction received, on reaching
the wide thoroughfare of St. Giles' Brian parked

the car among the line of other vehicles. After receiving a ticket from the attendant, he and Pamela started off on foot along Broad Street on their way to the address in Holywell.

They reached the house and rang the bell. The door was opened by a big man with greying hair and a clipped moustache. Brian gave his name.

"You're punctual," came the reply. "Come along in." He glanced questioningly at Pamela.

"Are you Detective Inspector Copthorne?" Brian asked. Getting a reply in the affirmative, he introduced Frank's sister, saying she had wanted to come too.

Copthorne did not seem annoyed as Brian had half expected he might be. "All the better," he said. He led the way into a room where comfortable chairs stood round a bright fire. "This house belongs to a friend of mine," he went on, "and I felt it would be the least public place for us to meet. Now sit down, and tell me first how Tilney is."

They did so, after which the inspector asked Brian to give a detailed account from the beginning, that is, from the time of the tea-shop incident. Pamela also spoke of the parts she knew. At the end various questions were asked to clear up certain points.

"Tilney, you tell me," said Copthorne presently, "insists that he was deliberately pushed into that old well you describe. Can we however be certain of that? When a chap's had a bad fall, his memory's apt to be a bit confused."

"That was my first idea," admitted Brian. "But on the other hand the man Budgeon was around. I recognised him before we started to follow, and I'm certain he was the same chap that Tilney identified in the tea-shop. Then again there was the matter of the torch being chucked away into the bushes. Not seeing it delayed us in finding Tilney, which was no doubt what the attacker intended, so as to gain more time to disappear."

"I agree," said Copthorne with a nod. "Also I can confirm to a certain extent that Budgeon was in your area. We know a good deal about him that's not to his credit, and, as he is a man we keep tabs on, as we say, we are well aware that he's been on holiday recently from the place where he works. He was due to clock in again at 8 a.m. this morning; he did, for I took the trouble to check that by 'phone a few minutes ago. At the same time that doesn't prove he wasn't in Kinford during the early hours of last night."

The inspector paused to pull out a pipe and light it. Then he went on.

"There would be no difficulty in finding some petty charge against Budgeon, so that we could pull him in for questioning; but that would get us no

6

further. It would simply put him even more on the alert, and perhaps make things more difficult over getting the man we so badly want, the one who is behind all this. Tilney reported to me on the 'phone the other day his idea that a Mr. Lethwick, who lives in your village, might be he, and suggested checking back on his record, and what sort of life he had led before coming to Kinford."

"Did you find out anything?" asked Pamela.

"Rather to my surprise, we did. Bit of a shady character by all accounts. Manager of a business in London which went broke, and there was a strong suspicion that he had been making a nice thing out of it. Nothing could actually be proved against him, but that probably explains why he thought it advisable to shift his quarters to the country. Now I'll tell you something else."

"Yes?" said Brian.

"In getting a line on Lethwick we also got a hint on that man of his, the fellow Romsey who got run over the other day. Now Romsey was a queer character—petty crime was his line, varied at times by turning 'coppers' nark'—in other words, giving surreptitious information to the police when it happened to suit his book. I have no idea, of course, whether Lethwick knew this, but it's suggestive."

"You mean that supposing Lethwick is really the 'X' you want to find, Romsey was a potential danger

to him.   He might find out too much, and——"
Brian broke off suddenly and pursed his lips in a
silent whistle.

" 'And'," Copthorne prompted.

"At the inquest the doctor wouldn't swear he'd
been run over.   He admitted that the injuries might
have been caused by other means.   In fact village
gossips, the good lady who comes up to work at Slad
Cottage in particular, hinted that the verdict was by
no means a true one."

"Exactly, and we won't lose sight of that, despite
the coroner's findings.   Now to go back to Budgeon.
On the assumption he was in your area 'on business,'
we must presuppose that 'X' is a neighbour of yours.
Leaving out Lethwick for the moment, what other
educated people are there living in and around your
village?"

Pamela was able to help there.   She gave quite
a list, including Mr. Quaintance, the vicar, and the
owner of the Manor.

"You pays your money and you takes your
choice!" quoted Inspector Copthorne with a smile,
"though I'll admit your friend Lethwick sounds the
most probable at the moment."

"Well, what do you propose to do?   Send down
a detective to nose round?" asked Brian.

"I could, but I can't see that he would find out
anything.   A country village is not like a town,

where you can tail a suspect easily. Everybody would know in ten minutes there was something phoney about him, however much he pretended to be a commercial traveller or an artist looking for winter scenes to sketch!"

"That's true," said Brian. "We two, with a definite reason for being about the village, could probably find out more. We could get old Nix to talk, not to mention the Tilney's gossiping housekeeper."

Copthorne nodded. "Yes, you might, provided you do it carefully. Report to me about anything you may discover, however trivial. And if something turns up that needs immediate and urgent action, get in touch at once with your local police headquarters. Let's see, Kinford's inside the borders of Gloucestershire, isn't it? Well, I'll get in touch with the county police, so that they'll know all about the case in the event of your wanting them in a hurry."

Seeing that the interview was at an end, Brian and Pamela rose to their feet.

Inspector Copthorne also got up. "You mustn't think," he said, "that I'm not doing anything because I don't arrange to send a dozen sleuths creeping round your village looking for clues. There's a lot that can be done which is not actually on the spot. In the meantime I'm very glad to have had this talk with you both. Remember me to your brother, Miss Tilney, and say I hope he gets fit again soon.   If this house were mine I'd ask you both to lunch, but as it is——"

"Oh, that's quite all right, thanks.   We'll get some in the town before we start back."

"One word more," added Copthorne as he shook hands.   "Be careful, you two.   If, as we suspect, an attempt was made on Tilney's life, and that Romsey's accident gives food for thought, someone might wonder if you might possibly know a bit more than you should.   Not that I think there's really any danger, but don't go giving needless opportunities, such as strolling about in the dark alone or forgetting to lock up at night!"

The two left the house and made their way towards the centre of the city.   They had not gone many yards before a rough-looking loafer, who had been idling on the pavement with his hands in his pockets, decided to move in the same direction.

Brian and Pamela turned into Cornmarket Street and entered a restaurant in search of lunch.   When they had finished their meal, Pamela took the opportunity to do some shopping.   They felt that there was no need to hurry home, for Frank was being well looked after in hospital, and there was plenty of time to get back before the daylight began to fade.

Carrying their various purchases they returned to where they had left the car.   Brian tipped the park-attendant, and got in.   He started the engine, and the two drove off along the homeward road.

Oddly enough, the same man who had been loafing outside the house where Copthorne had been, was now hanging about near the car-park, ostensibly engaged in picking up cigarette-ends that departing motorists had thrown away, and putting them in his pocket for future use.   With a sour grin on his lips he watched Brian and Pamela go off.   Then he spat out the sodden end of a cigarette he was smoking, and made his way to one of the telephone call-boxes that stand near the Martyrs' Memorial.

CHAPTER VII

A NARROW SHAVE

WHEN Brian and Pamela reached the outskirts of Oxford they ran into fog. It rolled white and dense across the low ground to the north of the city, and slowed their progress to a crawl. Cars coming in the opposite direction loomed up suddenly, their side-lights gleaming like the eyes of strange monsters. Brian found his work cut out to keep on the road at all, for at times the left-hand verge was almost invisible through the swirling vapour.

"I hope to goodness this will lift soon," he said, as a bump told him he had touched the kerb. "Otherwise it'll be anybody's guess when we'll get back."

"If there's any fog about it's always bad here near the canal. Once we're out of the Thames valley we're almost certain to run clear of it," replied Pamela encouragingly.

She was right. After travelling three or four miles at almost a walking pace, they found the whiteness beginning to thin. Then abruptly they passed out of it, and into the pale afternoon sunlight slanting across the countryside.

Brian switched off his side-lights and quickened speed. "That's better," he said with relief. "I was beginning to think we'd be still on the road when it gets dark. Fog is bad enough in the daytime, but it's the limit after nightfall!"

The miles rolled away under the wheels. They came to less frequented roads, and the cars they met became few and far between.

They reached a length of dead-straight road, a mile or so short of the place where they would have to turn off into the lanes for Kinford. In the distance a lorry was visible, apparently approaching at a very leisurely pace. It was a big green vehicle—one of those heavy affairs with a bow like a battleship and spanned by a massive bumper six inches wide.

The intervening gap lessened, and at the same time the lorry increased its speed, pounding forward along the crown of the road.

Brian hooted sharply. Instead of pulling over to its correct side the lorry swayed in the opposite direction and bore straight down on his small car. Brian realised that if he was not quick there would be an almighty smash.

He wrenched the steering-wheel over, and with a bump the car mounted the left-hand grass verge. The next instant the lorry passed over the spot where the little car would have been had not its driver acted as he did.

Brian had been travelling at a good speed, but he managed to keep his ill-used car from turning over, and from crashing into the loose-stone wall bordering the verge. He pulled up, his wheels skidding on the wet grass. Meanwhile the lorry which had caused the trouble was rapidly disappearing in the distance.

"What the blazes was that fellow doing?" exclaimed Brian. "That was a lot too close to a near thing to my liking!" he added, glancing at Pamela beside him.

Her face was white, but beyond that she showed no signs of shock. She had not even cried out when an appalling smash seemed inevitable. Brian had liked her before, but now she went up in his estimation with a bound, especially as he felt his own hands shaking slightly from the after-effects.

"Inspector Copthorne's warning to us wasn't exaggerated," she said calmly. "That was deliberate."

Brian agreed, in forceful language. "I wish I'd been quick enough to spot the number," he continued.

"You couldn't have done. The number-plate was plastered with mud so as to make it quite unreadable. They'll probably stop and wash it off at the next stream."

"Could you make out anything of the chap who was driving?"

Pamela shook her head. "He had a cap pulled down low and a muffler round his chin—he didn't mean to risk any chance of being identified later. If it hadn't been for your presence of mind, Brian, we'd have been killed."

Except for a nod, Brian made no reply to that obvious statement. He stepped out of the car to see if anything was bent or broken before attempting to regain the road. As he did so he realised that there was an unanswered question puzzling him, and as he took his seat again he spoke of it to Pamela.

"That was intentional, that attempt to run us down, but how did the fellows, whoever they were, know we'd reach here just when we did, and be dawdling along expecting us?"

"More than I can say, but if Mr. Lethwick is at the bottom of all this, didn't we meet him this morning? He knew we'd gone into Oxford, and would be coming out. Others probably knew as well, for Mrs. Pratley isn't exactly dumb, and she'd talk when she went back to the village at midday."

"True. But the exact timing still puzzles me."

The girl shrugged. "We're up against clever

people. Now what about getting on again if there's no damage done?"

Brian worked the car back on to the road. He turned presently into the lane that led to the village, his thoughts busy with the implications connected with what had happened. He glanced towards his companion, and spoke.

"I'm a bit worried about you," he said. "Under the circumstances, wouldn't it be better if you didn't stay on at Slad Cottage? I mean these people may be up to some more dirty work before long."

"They're not going to scare me away!" Pamela retorted with spirit. "I'm going to see this through. It's not as if I were there alone. You're on the spot, and we'll have Frank back tomorrow. We'll just have to be careful we're not caught off our guard, that's all."

Brian said no more. He felt in a way that the girl's pluck was a challenge to himself. If she meant to see it through, so would he, and any consequences could go hang! He realised that, with Frank disabled, he would now have to take a leading part in the game of collecting information on which the inspector could act. He might get knocked out as a result, but the fact that there was danger attached to it made the prospect all the more attractive.

In due course they reached their destination. The key was under the stone slab where Mrs. Pratley had put it when she finished her work and went off home.   But almost as soon as Brian and Pamela had entered the cottage they realised that someone must have known or guessed where she had hidden that key.   There were faint traces of damp footmarks on the freshly polished linoleum, and several small articles were not in their usual positions.

"What the deuce could the intruder have been after?" said Brian, frowning.   "I suppose Frank hadn't any papers or records of his recent work that might be useful to what we'll call 'the enemy'?"

Pamela shook her head.   "Never anything like that here, I'm certain.   I can't imagine why anyone should want to prowl round while we were away. Except some tramp, of course, but then nothing seems to have been stolen."

"Oh well, perhaps it was some hopeful snooper wanting to know the number of bedrooms before applying for the next tenancy!"   Brian spoke lightly, but he felt that the incident was significant all the same, in spite of the fact that it seemed so pointless. But this, like the incident of the lorry, ought to be reported to Copthorne, who had said he wanted to be told of any circumstance, however trivial.

"As soon as Frank is back we shall have to set about thinking out a plan of campaign," said Brian as he and Pamela were eating their breakfast next morning. "Not that Frank will be able to take any active part, but three heads are better than two. When did they say we were to fetch him from the hospital?"

"Any time after lunch," Pamela replied. "We might as well go along as soon as we've had ours."

"Yes, that'll be best. In the meantime I'll be around. Give you a hand in the house, if you like."

"Nothing doing!" retorted Pamela with a grin. "Mrs. Pratley will be here, remember, and she'll stand no amateur interference! She'd say she was put upon—no, 'wronged' is her expression."

"I'll go and tinker with the car instead, then. I want to give it a good look over, and make sure we didn't crack a spring yesterday when we bumped up on to the roadside. By the way, Mrs. P. will talk, as she always does, so you might get some useful pickings about people round here which Inspector Copthorne would like to have."

"Oh, I'll be on the look-out," said Pamela as she rose from the table. "One of the first things I want to find out is if she saw anybody hanging around here yesterday, who might have seen where she put that key, and taken the opportunity to have a snoop round."

Pamela had no luck in this, however. She brought the conversation round tactfully, and without mentioning that the house had been entered, but apparently Mrs. Pratley had not seen anyone. If the intruder had been lingering in the vicinity, waiting for her to go, he had kept himself well hidden.

In due course Brian and Pamela reached the hospital without incident. Frank was already dressed and waiting for them, his arm enormous in its plaster casing and supported by a sling round the neck.

One of the first questions he asked when they had settled him comfortably in the back seat of the car, with Pamela beside him, was about the result of the interview with Inspector Copthorne, which Frank knew was to take place after their visit to the hospital on the previous day.

Brian left it to Pamela to tell him the gist, while he himself concentrated on his driving. In parts the road was none too good, and he wanted to avoid bumping Frank unnecessarily. Behind him he could hear the girl's voice describing to her brother what Copthorne had said, and also giving an account of the narrow escape they had had when driving home afterwards.

They reached Slad Cottage. Pamela was all for getting Frank to lie down and rest, but he was not having any. *"That's* what I've been looking forward to seeing!" he said with a gesture of his sound left arm towards the bright fire in the sitting-room.

"No bedroom for me—I'll be a lot more comfortable in an easy chair with my feet on the fender! Thanks," he went on as Brian helped him to sit down. "I've not got used yet to being one-handed, and the weight of this plaster on the other arm makes me feel all lop-sided." He sank back with a contented sigh and added, "Pamela gave me a general sketch of events as we came along in the car; now let's have the whole bag o' tricks."

Between them Brian and Pamela gave him a detailed account.

"It seems that warning Copthorne gave you wasn't out of place," he commented when they had finished. "About that recklessly driven lorry, I mean. As I've always known, we're up against a tough lot. That being so, I think I ought to send Pamela home to our people, before any more funny business happens."

"I've already suggested that," put in Brian, "but she won't have it."

"Certainly I'm not going to run away, especially with you laid up, Frank," retorted Pamela. "I'm staying here, and that's flat!"

Frank shrugged. "Pig-headed. But you always have been that, my girl! Anyway, we'll shelve that point for the moment. The situation boils down to this. Though admittedly it's only surmise that Lethwick is 'X', he is definitely first suspect.

According to Copthorne, his past is not too credit-
able, and his manservant Romsey is known to have
had a criminal record.   Added to that is the fact
that we saw him and Budgeon, with heads together,
in that tea-shop, despite the fact that he went out of
his way to deny to you, Brian, that he had ever met
the fellow before.   At the same time Copthorne
realises that to send a detective down here to watch
his movements would defeat its own object, for a
stranger in the village would rouse suspicion at once.
Curse it that I'm out of the running with this arm!"
Frank added angrily.   "I've had the training and
I'm here on the spot—but there it is!"

"When we had our talk with Copthorne it was
suggested that the village people might be a source
of information," said Brian.   "I said we'd try to
find out anything we could, and let him know."

Frank shrugged.   "Doubt if it would be a very
profitable line, but there's no reason why it shouldn't
be tried.   Lethwick's not only a comparative newcomer but a man they dislike; probably ninety per
cent of what they might say would be just gossip
with no foundation of truth.   Still, it can be tried,
provided you do it carefully."

The discussion continued, the point not being
forgotten that they might be working on an entirely
wrong assumption and that "X" might not be Lethwick at all.   Frank's conclusion was that only having

Budgeon tailed by an expert the next time he left London for the country would be really effective. "And that's Copthorne's job to arrange," he ended.

"All the same, it's up to us to pull our weight at this end as Copthorne asked us," Brian persisted. "Pamela can see if she can filter anything useful out of Mrs. Pratley's chatter, and I could have a shot at getting old Nix on the talk. I've a ready-made excuse for going to find him; I can tell him you want to know, Frank, when he's coming to fill in that old well, as he promised. That'll have to wait till morning, though," he added, glancing out of the window to where the winter darkness was gathering. Copthorne's warning about being out alone in the dark had not been forgotten.

CHAPTER VIII

THE BROKEN FLASK

IN the morning, under a sky of scurrying clouds driving before a rising wind, Brian set out on foot for the village.

It was only when he was entering it he remembered that Frank had never explained exactly where to find Nix's cottage. However, that was easily remedied; he would ask for directions at the village shop.

As he approached it, to his surprise he saw emerge the same girl he had previously met there. Goodman's niece, Miss Sybil Kelly, the shopman had said she was. Her attention was occupied in looking in her bag for her purse so as to put away some change. A moment later the coins slipped from her hand and went rolling this way and that.

"Don't worry—I'll help!" cried Brian with a laugh as he neatly fielded one of the spinning coins. "Here's another—we'll have 'em all back where they belong in a jiffy!"

The girl thanked him as she held out her hand

for the cash he had collected, and made as if to move on.   Brian spoke again.

"We met the other day in the shop, and the owner told me who you were."   Brian mentioned his own name, and added that he was staying at Slad Cottage with the Tilneys.

"I remember seeing you there—a new face is such a rarity in Kinford," replied Sybil with a faint smile. "I've heard of your friends, but I've never met them. Hasn't Mr. Tilney recently had a bad accident?"

"Yes, but he's home again now, and his sister and I are looking after him.   At least she is, mainly," said Brian more accurately.

"Yes, I expect that is so."   Sybil smiled again and added, "Thanks once more for picking up the money."   She turned to move on.

"Just a moment!" Brian interposed.

"Yes?"   The girl stopped.

"You said just now you hadn't met the Tilneys, but you will.   Mr. Goodman has asked us to come up to the Manor one day soon, and I know Pamela wants to meet you.   Frank, I'm afraid, won't be able to go out yet awhile, however."

"Oh, if you know Uncle, and he's asked her—and you too, I hope—that will be splendid!" said Sybil eagerly, her face lighting up. The slightly nervous expression had vanished, and Brian now saw that she was really pretty. "Up at the Manor I hardly see anyone—Uncle doesn't entertain, you see, and——" She broke off as if afraid to say too much.

"Well, you'll be seeing Pamela—and me too if you can bear it!"

"I'll try!" Sybil retorted with a laugh. "And now I must really be getting on."

Brian watched her slim figure retreating along the street. "To-day's good deed!" he said to himself. "I believe I've cheered the poor girl up quite a lot. Must be a dull life up at the Manor from all accounts. Besides, it's broken the ice, and made things easier for Pamela when she goes up to call." It was not until Sybil was almost out of sight that he remembered that he could have asked her the way to Nix's cottage. With a sigh at his forgetfulness, he entered the shop to obtain the directions he wanted.

He found the place without difficulty. The stooping and white-haired Mrs. Nix opened the door. "My 'usband, 'e's at work," she replied to Brian's question. "If you wants 'em, 'e's up at the top end o' Mr. Gorringe's ten-acre medder, seein' to one o' them walls."

Brian remembered that Nix had said he had another job before he could return to Frank's place and see to the filling of the well. He asked how to get there.

Mrs. Nix's explanation might have been clear

enough to a local man, but to a stranger like Brian it was puzzling. However, he gathered that if he went a short way back along the slad road, cut across the fields to his left, and headed towards the woods that ran along the crest of the high ground behind Frank's cottage, he would come on Nix somewhere along the loose-stone wall that divided the trees from the open wold.

He carried on accordingly. In due course he left the road and took to the fields which, as he breasted the slope, gave place to rough grazing-ground. Overhead the ragged grey clouds were sweeping across the sky, for the wind that had been blowing since daylight was steadily increasing in strength.

Brian neared the long line of trees, their bare branches rocking and groaning in the rising gale. Under their screen the force of the wind was less. He halted, looking to right and left, but could see no sign of Nix. Having decided which way to turn, he moved along parallel with the wall for two or three hundred yards, and then caught sight of a distant figure at work beside a scree of fallen stones.

Nix greeted Brian's arrival with a broad grin. "Oo'd 'a' thought o' seein' you 'ere, mister? You come for to give me an 'and with this 'ere job?"

Brian laughed. "I wouldn't mind, though I'd be a fat lot of use. The stones would probably tumble down as fast as I put 'em up!"

"Ah. Reckon they would. You got to know this 'ere job proper. Fifty year I been at it, an' I've summat to learn yet."

Brian brought up the subject of when Nix was coming to fill in the old well.

"I ent forgot. Reckon I shall finish this 'ere come tea-time, an' I'll be along termorrer early for to make a start. 'Ow's Mr. Tilney farin'? They tell me 'e's 'ome again."

"That's right. He's getting on well, though he finds things awkward with only one arm, and a heavy plaster as big as a pillow on the other."

"Ah, they fixed things different time I was a boy. Couple o' slats off a wooden box, strapped up tight, was good enow for us them days."

"You must have seen a lot of changes in these parts," remarked Brian, hoping to encourage Nix to talk. "New buildings, new people, and so on."

"Ah." Nix paused to fit a large stone neatly into its chosen place. "New folk, mostly. There ent been a lot o' new houses—village is much the same as what I remembers as a youngster. Barrin', o' course, what that there Lethwick ha' shoved up. We could ha' done without that—an' without 'im too, comin' round an' talkin' down to us folks as if we was a pack o' fools."

Brian laughed.

"Ah," Nix went on. "Now if it was the Reverend

Quaintance up at the Vicarage we wouldn't ha' minded a lot, seeing that's expected, like, in 'is job; but 'e don' 'ardly ever leave 'is study. Bookish, if you takes my meanin'. But that there Lethwick—ah!"

"Yes, I've gathered he's not liked. Still, I suppose he has some friends."

"Ah, Lunnon folk what comes occasional in big cars. I've seen 'em. Some on 'em wearin' di'mond rings an' big cigars stickin' in their faces, same as what 'e does 'imself. I wouldn't trust them sort with sixpence o' mine." Nix spat to emphasise the point.

Brian waited while some more stones were set in the rising fabric. Clearly Nix was in a mood to chat.

"Do yer know what?" he went on presently. "It wouldn't surprise me none if I was tole that there Lethwick 'adn't been up to no good afore 'e come 'ere. They say you can tell a man by the comp'ny 'e keeps. I ent 'ad no eddication but I knows a wrong-'un when I sees 'un. That Romsey, 'e was another. I wouldn't be surprised if there worn't summat rum about the way 'e got runned over. There's a new chap come now—Lethwick fetch 'im out from Oxford yesterday."

Brian remembered the man that he and Pamela had seen in the car at the pump-station.

Nix fixed another section of wall, and continued.

"Lethwick ent the sort we wants round 'ere. 'E ent like Mr. Goodman up at the Manor. 'E's a gent, now. Stan Dawson, what's head cowman there, 'e says 'e's an easy master to work for." Nix went on to speak of the pedigree stock under Dawson's charge, and the way they won prizes at shows. "Interested in old things too, what gets dug up, Mr. Goodman is," he added.

Brian mentioned that Goodman had already spoken to him of his prehistoric finds in the district.

"Ah. There's a won'erful lot o' them old tumps round 'ere, where folks was buried thousands o' year back."

Brian nodded. He had heard there were many ancient tumuli and barrows of Stone and Bronze Age man still to be traced on the hilltops.

"Four or five years ago," Nix went on, "some gents come down from Lunnon for to go an' dig over yonder at Black Knapp. They wanted to hire chaps from the village, but none of 'em would take it on, and in the end they hire Lunnon workmen. They found a kind o' underground room built o' big slabs o' stone, with a lot o' bones an' other things what they took away to shove in museums an' suchlike. They give Mr. Goodman some on 'em—it was part o' 'is land they was diggin'."

"Why couldn't they get local men as helpers?" asked Brian.

Nix carefully fitted some more stones into the wall, and ignored the question. This roused Brian's interest, and he repeated it.

"They didn't care about it. No, not even when the gents offer double wages," Nix replied at length. "It's reckoned mortal bad luck to meddle with them things."

"You mean they're supposed to be haunted?"

"Ah. Maybe it's just foolishness, like. Us folks don' mind goin' there daytime, but there's a lot in the village what wouldn't spend a night by one o' them tumps for untold gold. Dunno I'd care to meself. I've seen things, I 'ave. Time I've bin out on the wolds, settin' a few snares by moonlight, I've seen figgers standin' alongside that there tump on Black Knapp I was speakin' of. I ent easy scared, but I clear off quick. There's a lot o' things what ent natural," Nix ended with a shake of his head.

Brian had a feeling that he had at last got hold of something significant. If anyone in the neighbourhood wanted a spot that was safe from observation, where he could meet his lieutenants and issue instructions, there could be none better than one which was universally shunned at night by the local people. Even if they were seen, they would be taken for supernatural beings.

"I'd like to see this place you mention, where the archaeologists were digging," he said.

"Ah. It ent far." Nix straightened his back and pointed. "See the Manor down there?" He indicated the trees and buildings in the middle distance. "Now you see that big wold to the left an' beyond it?" There was a domed mass of high ground a mile farther on, with fields on the lower slopes and a bare grassy top. "That's Black Knapp, that is. If you looks careful you can see the tump like of a pimple on top. That's where they was diggin'."

"I think I'll go and have a look at it right away," said Brian.

"Ah, please yerself, though there ent a lot to see." As Brian turned to go, Nix added, "Tell Mr. Tilney I'll be along fust thing termorrer to do that there fillin'-in job."

Brian found that to reach the top of Black Knapp took him much longer than he expected. Stone walls, and in places thick-set hedges, barred his way across the intervening ground, and though the former could be climbed, the latter meant finding gates. Also many of the fields had been recently ploughed and were sticky with rain, and it was easier to go round them than to try to cross with many pounds of clinging earth weighing down his feet.

Halfway up the side of the big hill he passed clear of the part that had been brought under cultivation, and set foot on the grassy upper slopes. It proved easier walking, but he had another obstacle to contend against. On the lower levels he had not been so conscious of the wind, but on the exposed elevation he had now reached he met the full force of the westerly gale. It was difficult even to stand up against it as it swept round the hillside, and climbing the last ascent became a matter of sheer hard work.

At last he reached the brow and saw ahead of him the low grassy mound of the tumulus that Nix had pointed out from a distance. If he had not been told what it was, he would have thought it to be a natural irregularity crowning the smooth rounded crest of the wold.

Brian had no difficulty in finding the spot where the archaeologists had been digging four or five years previously. The heaps of earth which had been shovelled out still lay there, now weathered and weed-grown. Between them was the dark opening of the prehistoric grave that had been exposed.

He stepped up to it and peered inside. He could distinguish little beyond the fact that the sides and roof of the low entry were formed of rough slabs of grey Cotswold stone. Brian remembered that he had a box of matches in his pocket. He struck one of them, but the gale howling round the hilltop blew it out instantly. Bending double to clear the low roof, he crawled a little way inside. Here he struck a second match, and managed this time to keep it alight between his sheltering hands.

As Nix had said, there was nothing much to see. It was just a dank hole that penetrated into the mound for some distance. Whatever had been buried there had long since been removed by those modern and scientific tomb-robbers. Not a bone or a trinket of any sort which had once belonged to that neolithic chief remained where it had lain for so many centuries.

Brian expended another match. As he turned to crawl out of the cavity, the tiny flame he held reflected its light on something bright and polished lying at the base of the side wall. He picked it up and emerged into the daylight. His find was only a discarded thermos-flask, with pieces of the broken glass lining rattling about inside the outer case.

Nothing exciting or interesting about that, thought Brian. Or was there? It had certainly not been left behind by the archaeologists, for the metal was fresh and unrusted; had it belonged to them, it would by now have crumbled into oxide in that damp hole. Shepherds and other farm workers, he reflected, usually carry such things for their mid-day meal, though from the look of it, the flask he had found was of a far more expensive kind than they usually buy.

Also, if the place were more or less shunned by

the village folk even in the daytime, would one of them have chucked his broken property inside the very heart of the supposedly haunted spot? Surely he would toss it under the nearest bush, and not where it had just been found. That, together with the original quality of the article, pointed to the fact that it had belonged to some stranger to the district. One who had been there quite recently, too, and there are no trippers or hikers on the wolds in winter.

Brian saw at once that this helped to confirm the idea which had sprung into his mind as soon as Nix had mentioned vague figures standing by the tumulus in the moonlight.   It was almost proof that the spot was being used as a secret meeting-place, for there was no other reason for people to be there at that hour.   No doubt the flask had been brought to provide a hot drink while waiting on that cold and wind-swept hilltop.   When accidentally dropped, it had been tossed inside rather than left lying on the grass where it might be seen by some passing shepherd and make him wonder who had been there recently.

Another point occurred to Brian, and one of no little importance.   Up till now he and Frank and Pamela had been working on the conviction that Lethwick was the mysterious "X".   But was the crest of Black Knapp a likely spot for Lethwick to choose as a rendezvous?   Surely not.   Lethwick was essentially a townsman.   The betting was a thousand to one, therefore, that if he wanted to arrange a general meeting he would pick on some more-or-less civilised place; such as a private room at an inn, or indeed a tea-shop of the kind where Brian and Frank had seen him talking to Budgeon.

Supposing Lethwick were eliminated, who else could it be?   The answer was an easy one.   Barring Goodman and the Vicar, there was nobody of sufficient education to fill the rôle in Kinford; but there must be several with the estimated qualifications in neighbouring villages that lay within easy reach of Black Knapp.   Pamela had given Inspector Copthorne quite a list.   The night that Budgeon had been seen and followed, he might have been going to or from one of those nearby houses.

Having reached this conclusion, Brian set about making a more thorough search of the vicinity of the tumulus.   He discovered nothing more, however.   Nor were there any footmarks visible on the short hard turf that lay like a skin above the solid rock of the wold.   He realised that there was nothing more he could do at the moment; the next thing was to return to Slad Cottage and discuss the outcome of his morning's walk with Frank.   He tucked the broken flask under his arm, and started off down the wind-swept hillside.

The two at the cottage greeted Brian's return with some relief. Owing to having had to hunt for Nix, and the added delay of his expedition to Black Knapp, he had been absent much longer than they had expected, and they were beginning to wonder if another "accident" had occurred. Brian reported his doings fully and from the start, including his meeting with Sybil Kelly, and at the end produced for inspection the broken flask he had found on Black Knapp.

Both Frank and Pamela confirmed the idea that it had not been discarded by some farmworker. "They stick to the cheaper kind," said the former, "which is quite good enough for their purpose and doesn't cost very much to replace in case it gets smashed. I agree, too, with your theory about Lethwick—it's not the sort of place he'd be likely to choose for a meeting. At the same time we can't be in any way positive about that."

Brian expressed his idea about someone from a neighbouring village.

Frank nodded. "It's quite on the cards you may be right. You tell me Nix actually saw figures waiting there when he was out doing a spot of poaching by moonlight. Did he say exactly when he saw them?"

"No, why? Is it important?"

"Might be. If it's a periodical rendezvous, and

we knew past dates, we might calculate when it is likely to be used again and set a watch. It seems the quickest way to find out who 'X' really is."

"I'd thought of that already. I could see Nix again and ask him about the times."

"Probably better if I did that," replied Frank. "If he's coming here to-morrow on that well-filling job, I could get him to come in and have a chat with me."

CHAPTER IX

TWO VISITS

"WHILE we're waiting for Frank to have his heart-to-heart talk with Nix," Pamela remarked to Brian next morning, "what's wrong with the idea of going up to the Manor and making our promised call on your girl friend?"

"Nothing that I can see," Brian replied. "I'm certain she'd appreciate it, and I said you'd be going soon. I suppose Frank will be all right while we're away?"

"Of course I shall!" put in the invalid. "I shall have Mrs. P. here, not to mention Nix. Anyone would think I was entirely helpless!"

"Well you are, pretty nearly, and we're taking no chances of any more funny business," retorted his sister. "We're managing this, so you shut up!"

"All right, all right—Nix'll be better company than you are!" Frank answered back with a grin. "He'll probably cheer me up by giving me lurid details of other accidents, such as people falling off harvest wagons or being cut to ribbons by mower-knives, that have happened during the last fifty years!"

"Mind the excitement of listening to his yarns doesn't make you forget what you are going to ask him about Black Knapp!" laughed Brian.

"You needn't be afraid of that. I'll have something to tell you in exchange for any titbits of interest you may hear up at the Manor. And don't forget to look intelligent, Brian, when Goodman shows you his collection of bits and pieces—if you can, that is!" Frank made an airy gesture of dismissal with his sound hand. "Personally, prehistoric relics and things of that sort bore me stiff, though I naturally didn't say so to Goodman when he spoke about them."

The high wind had eased off during the night, and had been followed by gusty rain. The first idea was that Pamela and Brian should walk to the Manor, but before starting they changed their minds. There was no point in getting wet and arriving in dripping mackintoshes; besides, with a car they would be able to return more quickly.

By the time they turned into the drive, with its long avenue of bordering trees, the rain had temporarily eased. It was the first time Brian had seen the big grey house of Cotswold stone at close quarters. It had a typical early Georgian frontage, with tall windows between pilasters rising from ground to eaves, and a pillared portico projecting over the front door. A glimpse of one side of the building, however, indicated that the frontage was a later addition grafted on to a much earlier period, when Tudor architecture became unfashionable among country squires.

Brian stopped the car. He and Pamela got out, mounted the steps and rang the bell. They waited, and rang again. At length the door opened and a figure in the garb of a butler appeared. He was fat and pasty-faced, and his bulk filled even the wide doorway. This, Brian reflected, must be the male half of the man-and-wife staff which he had been told Goodman employed to manage his housekeeping. He did not think much of the squire's choice, but then domestic staff is hard to come by these days.

"Mr. Goodman is absent from home," was the announcement the visitors received. "He left early this morning to attend a cattle sale at Hereford."

This was unexpected, though Brian guessed that it might give his companion a better chance of getting to know Sybil Kelly if her uncle were not around. Pamela's reply to the statement about Goodman was to ask for the girl instead.

"She also is not at home," replied the man, standing immovable in the doorway. He said it in a tone which implied that it was a formal way of saying "No admittance during the owner's absence".

It looked to Pamela and Brian as if their journey was going to be for nothing. They were about to turn back towards the car when Sybil appeared round the corner of the house. She wore gumboots and a dirty mackintosh, and was carrying a bucket that appeared to have contained hen-food.

She pulled up with a jerk and seemed as if about to retreat. Then recognising Brian, and guessing who his companion was, she came forward. Pamela promptly descended the steps and advanced, holding out her hand. The fat butler gave a perceptible shrug, as if implying that he had done his best and was in no way to blame, and disappeared from sight, leaving the door ajar.

"Uncle isn't here," said Sybil as she shook hands. "He doesn't—I mean you won't be able to see the things he's found—the collection, you know—that you said he'd asked you to see," she said confusedly to Brian. "He keeps the room locked up."

"No matter, another time will do," said Brian, while Pamela put in: "Well, we can at least see you —that's what I've come for anyway!" Realising that she would have to take the initiative, she added, "Won't you ask us in?"

"Oh sorry, I'm forgetting my manners entirely these days! I suppose it's from seeing so few people. Yes, of course come in." Sybil made a gesture towards the door which the butler had abandoned.

"Go ahead and lead the way!" said Pamela. "I'm sure you and I will find plenty to talk about, even though Brian won't be able to have a look at the old bones and stuff, whatever it is." As they climbed the steps she slipped her arm through that of Sybil.

Brian took the hint. As Goodman was absent, he saw he would be in the way. The two girls would get to know each other far quicker if he were not there, an unnecessary third. "As there is no chance of seeing the collection," he said, "would you mind, Miss Kelly, if I strolled on towards the farm-buildings to see the cattle? I've always been interested, and——" He broke off, not quite knowing how to finish this hardly truthful statement.

Pamela shot him a glance of approval as she disappeared inside the house, still propelling Sybil. Brian picked up the bucket which the girl had dropped in the middle of the drive, placed it out of anybody's way, and then strolled onwards in the direction of the sheds that housed the pedigree stock.

There were several men about, and one of them, with a look of authority, advanced towards Brian to ask his business. Brian explained how he came to be there, and remembering what he had heard the previous day, added, "Are you Mr. Dawson? Nix was speaking about you to me yesterday."

The head cowman's expression cleared. "Ah, that's me. So you knows old Charlie? I mind now he telled me of a visitor come recent to the cottage up the slad. How's Mr. Tilney farin'? He's out o' hospital now, I understand."

"Yes, he's back, though of course he'll have to take things pretty quietly for some weeks till that arm of his is properly mended." They spoke for a minute or two about Frank, and when a pause came Brian mentioned the cattle. "I wonder if I might look round," he added. "I know Mr. Goodman's out, but I don't expect he'd mind."

"Ah. O' course he wouldn't. You ent one o' these here blighters what comes snoopin' round, tryin' to find out what we're sendin' to shows and such-like. I'll take you along, willin'." Dawson's pleasure at the interest in his charges showed in his face.

He led the way to the nearest of the long low buildings. With the air of a practised showman he conducted Brian along the rows of stalls, halting beside each well-bred beast they contained and describing at length its pedigree and the various prizes and cups that some of them had won. He was certainly an enthusiast over his job.

"Bein' winter-time, we has to keep 'em under cover and feed 'em high," Dawson went on to explain. "Come summer, o' course, they're out in the open, and then there ent half the same work attached to lookin' after 'em. Except them as what's goin' to be shown, that is—they needs a lot o' extry feedin' an' groomin', they do. But mostly they stops out in the fields time the weather's warm."

"Do you ever take them up Black Knapp to graze?" asked Brian. "I believe it's part of Mr. Goodman's land? Nix told me yesterday about that queer old place on the top, and I climbed up there afterwards to have a look at it."

"Ah, sometimes we does. The grass ent bad early summer, though it get poor and dry quick on that there high ground. None of 'em ent been there since the end o' June time."

That, Brian reflected, settled the possibility of the broken flask being left by one of Goodman's employees in attendance on the cattle. He hoped that Dawson might make some comment about the tumulus he had mentioned, and even refer to what Nix claimed to have seen there; but the head cowman was clearly not interested in either relics of the past or the possibility of ghostly visitors in the present.

They moved on once more. As they were crossing a yard Brian caught sight of a large green lorry parked there. It looked familiar, somehow, with its heavy front and broad bumper. Then it struck him that it was extremely like, in shape and colour, to the one which had nearly run down himself and Pamela on the journey back from Oxford. Of course there were probably a number of similar ones about, but still—— Certainly the number-plate of this one was clean enough, and easy to read at a distance.

"Is that yours?" he asked, pointing to the vehicle.

"That's right. We uses her for fetchin' feedin'-stuffs what we ent able to grow ourselves on the estate."

"I think I saw it on the road the other day." Brian mentioned the time and place.

Dawson shook his head. "You couldn't ha' done. And for why, it wasn't took out. Mr. Goodman he don' let nobody drive her but me, and I was havin' a day off time you speaks about, the missus bein' poorly and me stoppin' home to help with the childer."

"Oh well, then, I must be mistaken." The similarity however continued to intrigue him. "I suppose," Brian added, "that nobody could have taken her out without your knowledge?"

"Well, now, it's a rum-'un you should say that, mister. Time I was back at work next day one o' them tyres was flat, and I could ha' sworn there was naught wrong with 'em the day before."

"Still, if somebody had been using her without leave, your men here would have noticed," Brian commented.

"Well, happen she wasn't standing where she be

now, but up the lane yonder, behind them trees. I left her there time I finish work, and go straight back to my cottage. I meant to fetch her back early nex' mornin', and then what with the missus bein' poorly——"

Dawson broke off, considering, and then went on. "I ent tellin' you a lie when I say some-'un *could* ha' took her unseen and put her back same place. Now I comes to think on it, time I use her again it seem to me there was less petrol in the tank than I'd reckoned. I'll see she stop right here in future time she ent bein' used; nobody can't take her then without half-a-dozen of us chaps spottin' him quick!"

Brian said no more, but what he had heard gave him something to think about. He felt pretty certain now that it was the same vehicle, taken surreptitiously by someone who had plastered mud over the number-plates to prevent identification, and then returned it undetected to its former position. Who the person could have been remained a mystery however; Pamela had seen only a muffled figure behind the wheel, and one impossible to recognise.

Having seen all there was to see, Brian thanked Dawson for the trouble he had taken and strolled back to the front of the Manor. Pamela was not yet in sight, so presumably she was still somewhere inside with Sybil. He was not going to risk another dirty look from that butler and ask where they were;

instead he took his seat in the car and waited patiently. It was not until half an hour later that Pamela reappeared, accompanied by Sybil, who had now lost her look of shyness and appeared animated and jolly. Clearly Pamela's visit had done her a lot of good.

Brian started the engine and turned the car. As he drove out into the public road he glanced at his companion. "Well, how did you get on?" he asked. "Anything interesting to report?"

"Just a bit," Pamela answered. "What about you?"

"I've just a bit too," Brian replied. "If yours is equal to mine, we'll have quite a lot to tell Frank when we get back."

After Pamela and Brian had left for the Manor, Frank settled down by the fire to read. He found himself getting more used to his left-handed state, though it was annoying to have to lay down the book every time he wanted to turn a page. From outside he could hear occasionally the rumble of a wheelbarrow as Nix worked; in due course, Frank guessed, Nix would drift round to the back door in search of a cuppa, when he would ask him to come into the sitting-room and have a chat, and try to find out more details about those figures seen on Black Knapp.

Frank's reading was interrupted by Mrs. Pratley opening the door. " 'Ere's the Vicar come for to see you," she announced.

The Reverend James Quaintance entered. He was a stooping, white-haired man, with kindly eyes behind bifocal glasses. It was not difficult to guess that he lived alone, for his clerical clothes were badly in need of a visit to the cleaners.

"Don't get up! Please don't get up!" he exclaimed as Frank attempted awkwardly to rise. "I felt I had to call—somebody told me you hadn't been well. Oh yes, an accident, wasn't it?"

Frank lifted his plastered arm. "Most unfortunate—how did it happen?" the Vicar went on as he pulled forward a chair and sat down.

Frank gave his visitor an account of how he had come by his injury and his subsequent experiences in hospital, saying nothing of the real cause of his fall. As he spoke he realised that Mr. Quaintance was not taking in a quarter of what he was saying; the expression on his face showed clearly that his thoughts had wandered off on some journey of their own. When at last he made a remark, it had no connexion whatever with what Frank had been saying.

Frank saw that making conversation with his guest was going to be uphill work and, though appreciating that it was very kind of him to take the trouble to call, he hoped that he would not stay long.　Nor did he.　A few minutes later the Vicar rose to his feet.

"I must be going," he said.　"I hope you will be better soon.　An accident, wasn't it?　Yes, that's right—I seem to remember somebody telling me recently how it happened.　It's easy to let a knife slip when cutting things—you'll have to be more careful in future, my dear fellow."

Obviously what Frank had told him had not registered at all.　Mr. Quaintance gave his host a sympathetic smile and a pat on the shoulder, and took himself dreamily off—back to his beloved, and to most people boring, books and the fusty atmosphere of the vicarage study.

"Queer old bird!" said Frank to himself as he heard Mrs. Pratley's voice as she showed him out. "Still, it was decent of him to call, though by now he probably imagines he's just been to see someone who's down with influenza!　Nix will be less exasperating company; I think I hear him at the back door, and I'd better give Mrs. P. a shout and tell her I want to see him."

CHAPTER X

DISCUSSION

IN due course Brian and Pamela arrived back at Slad Cottage.

"You look cold," said Frank as they made straight for the fire and held out their hands to the blaze. "How did things go? Were you thrilled by the collection, and what was the niece like?"

"Mr. Goodman wasn't there, so we didn't see the prehistoric stuff," replied Pamela. "But I had quite a chat with the girl, while Brian went off on his own and filled in time making friends with the head cowman. What about Nix? Did you see him and find out what you wanted?"

"I did. But I can see you both have something up your sleeves to tell me, so my story can wait. Come on, Pamela—ladies first! Let's hear what you did."

"Really there's nothing very much to tell, though it interested me all the same," replied Frank's sister. "When we got there the butler came to the door with a 'no admittance, boss out' expression; but at that moment the niece appeared from somewhere round the back. She looked a trifle taken aback—perhaps she's afraid of that fat butler—but I swept her indoors before she quite knew what was happening.

"She said she'd take me up to her own rooms," Pamela went on. "To my surprise we had to mount miles and miles of stairs to where she has a bedroom and a tiny sitting-room on the top floor. Not uncomfortable, you know, but hardly the quarters one would have expected Mr. Goodman to allot to his niece, considering the amount of accommodation there is in that big house.

"Well, we sat and talked, and Sybil got over her shyness. She told me she's been at the Manor a couple of years, since her parents died, but obviously she doesn't find it too happy an existence. Apparently Mr. Goodman makes no attempt to see that she has friends of her own kind. No doubt he does what he thinks is his duty, but he doesn't understand the girl a bit. It struck me she's afraid of him. I expect he's dictatorial in his manner towards her—elderly bachelors absorbed in other things often are. Still, that's not going to put *me* off; I shall cultivate her acquaintance whenever I get a chance. She was quite cheered up when we came out to find Brian waiting patiently in the car. Now then, Brian—your turn!"

Brian looked at Frank and grinned. "I've found

the lorry that tried to run us down on the road back from Oxford, or at least I think I have!"

Frank sat up with a jerk. "What? At the Manor? Rubbish—you must be mistaken! From your description there are scores of that type of vehicle in use."

"Oh, I know that. But listen." Brian went on to describe what Dawson had said about the lorry he usually drove being left unattended in a by-lane on the date in question, and what he had admitted about the possibility of its having been taken and replaced without permission. "It seems to me," he went on, "that everything points to it being the same vehicle. Someone must have got to know that Dawson was off work that day, and where the lorry was parked, and pinched it for the job after defacing the number-plates with mud to prevent identification by any local man who might see it and wonder who was driving Dawson's particular lorry. It all hangs together."

Frank shrugged. "Maybe, but it doesn't get us further towards finding out who took it. Nor how anyone could know the time you'd be coming along that particular stretch of road."

"Unless we were recognised in Oxford and the time of our leaving 'phoned through to whoever's at the bottom of all this." Brian little knew how near he was to the mark. "For instance, we saw

Lethwick—he was coming out, I know, but he might have 'phoned back to someone in Oxford to watch out for us, let him know where we'd been, and when we left, so that he could take steps accordingly. Not that we are by any means sure, however, that Lethwick has anything to do with it. I am beginning very much to doubt it."

"It certainly wasn't Mr. Lethwick driving that lorry," Pamela put in. "The muffled figure I saw behind the wheel was short and stocky, and not Mr. Lethwick's build at all."

Silence fell between them. Presently Brian spoke again. "Leaving that for the present," he said, "did you find out anything from Nix, Frank?"

Frank stirred and shifted his position in his chair. "Yes, I saw Nix, and worked things round tactfully to Black Knapp and what you, Brian, told me he said to you about vague figures standing near that tumulus at night. I got out of him that he'd seen them more than once, and always on nights with a moon nearing the full. Recently in the autumn it was about 9 p.m. In the summer it was about midnight, and last Christmas it was much earlier—between six and seven."

"No fixed hour, in other words," said Brian.

"On the contrary, it seems to me that the times conform to a regular scale. That is, about two hours after sunset, depending on the season of the year."

"Then just now in mid-winter, when it gets dark soon after four in the afternoon, quite early in the evening would be the likely time?" put in Pamela.

"Exactly. I think we can take that as a fairly sound theory. Whoever these people are who meet at Black Knapp, presumably they start off as soon as dark sets in and need a couple of hours trekking by moonlight to get there. At least some of them do, so the time is fixed accordingly. Any from a distance may very well arrive at various points in the neighbourhood during the day, and converge on Black Knapp after nightfall. The major snag is that we have no idea whether it is a monthly rendezvous, or as and when occasion demands."

Brian nodded agreement, while Pamela remarked: "At least that gives something to work on. We could pick out a likely date and give the tip to the police to lie in wait and arrest anyone who turns up."

Frank turned scornfully on his sister. "On what charge?" he asked. "It's not a crime to stroll up a hill by moonlight and have a look at that relic of prehistoric man. Or to go there to look at the stars. Or to do a spot of ghost-hunting, having heard the local legend. We've got to know a lot more before any question of an arrest crops up. Besides, the

9

chaps we're up against aren't fools by any means; they'd know soon enough if the police were taking any interest in Black Knapp, and shun the place like the plague."

"Exactly what I was thinking," Brian observed. "The whole situation remains as it was, with the job of finding out something definite depending on us. Now let's see how we stand.   The next full moon is in four or five days' time, I believe, which means that the next few nights come under the heading of possibles, with the probability of the last three before the full.   That right?"

"Yes, according to what I got from Nix."

"Very well, then.   Somebody's got to be on the watch, and that's the job for me.   Starting tomorrow evening, say, I'll go and lie up there each night until the estimated period is over."

"Oh, Brian, is that wise?"   It was Pamela who spoke.   "What about Inspector Copthorne's warning about being out alone after dark?"

"I hadn't forgotten it, but there's no other alternative.   As a matter of fact it is you two I'm worrying about, in case any funny business starts here in my absence.   We don't want any more 'accidents'."

"Oh, we shall be all right," Pamela replied. "We'll lock up securely, and only open to let you in again when we hear your voice.   Besides, there's always the telephone in the event of any emergency."

"Very well then, that's what I'll do. Speaking of Copthorne," Brian went on, "I wonder if we ought to ring him up. He said we were to report anything that bore on the matter, however slight, so I think he ought to know about this Black Knapp idea. Will you do it, Frank, or shall I?"

"You'd better. He knows you now, since you met him in Oxford. Don't say more than you need —there's always an off-chance of somebody listening in at these rural exchanges."

Brian rose and crossed over to the instrument. He got through fairly quickly, and after saying who was speaking, reported the theory that had been formed about the possible meeting-place of the gang-boss and his lieutenants. He spoke guardedly and mentioned no names, but added that he himself proposed to take over the job of watching at the likely times and dates in the hope of identifying those who might assemble there.

"I don't altogether like it, but at the same time it's far the best solution. What bothers me is, if you're right in your theory, you'll be taking a big risk," was the reply.

"I don't mind that," said Brian.

"Maybe. But your relations might have a word to say to headquarters if you got scuppered! However, carry on and good luck to you. Now remember this." Copthorne's voice hardened to that of one used to command. "It's not your job to try accosting or anything like that; you're not a policeman and have no standing in the matter. What I want is a description of the persons who turn up at this possible meeting-place, with especial note of anyone you recognise as a local resident, together with anything you can manage to overhear. That last is vitally important. Then when the chance comes, slip off home and 'phone me. One thing more. Don't let yourself be seen; and if by any chance you are spotted, don't stop to argue but run like the devil!"

"Well, what did he say?" asked Frank and Pamela together as Brian put down the receiver.

"He seemed quite willing for me to have a try, though he sounded a bit worried in case I should land myself in a mess, up there alone. However, nothing may come of it in the end, and nobody may turn up."

"I agree with the Inspector," said Pamela. "I wish there could be two of you—I'd come myself and help to listen if it weren't for Frank."

"Of course you couldn't!" Brian retorted. "I'd chuck the whole thing rather than agree to your taking the risk of being beaten up!"

"Well, what about Mr. Goodman? It's his land. What about getting him to come in on this, Frank, and telling him in confidence the situation? He's

a local man, so it would not be a case of import-
ing a stranger whose arrival would arouse village
curiosity. Besides, he's a J.P., isn't he? I think
you said so once."

"I don't quite see where that last comes in," said
Frank. "A magistrate on the local bench isn't a
policeman. I suppose you mean that he's a respon-
sible person. Granted, but at the same time it's
quite impossible to take Goodman into our confidence. Copthorne would be furious if we acted in
this way without his permission, and I know I'm not
going to ask it and risk being told just where I get
off!"

"Nor am I sorry," concluded Brian. "We're
doing this off our own bat. No outsiders, I say,
until it comes to a show-down. That's my feeling
about it!"

CHAPTER XI

VIGIL ON BLACK KNAPP

BY the following morning Brian began to have some regrets about the impetuous way he had declared he would do the watching job on Black Knapp. He realised that lying out in mid-winter on the exposed hill-top, even for a limited period each night, was not going to be pleasant.

However, having said he would, he must carry on. He comforted himself with the reflection that it would only be for four or five evenings at most, for when the moon was past the full, according to the idea based on Nix's statement, those unknown persons were not likely to turn up there for another month. By that time his holiday would have long been over and himself back in London, and someone else could jolly well take it on!

Brian clothed himself for his first night's vigil in every garment he possessed, in addition to borrowing from Frank a pair of gumboots to pull over a couple of pairs of socks to keep his feet from being frozen. He had an early tea, and started out as dusk began to fall. This would give him an ample margin to be in position well before the estimated time when those who might be coming would arrive.

He had taken some thought about the best route to follow. The most direct way from Slad Cottage was by taking a track which passed near the Manor, but he felt he would be wise to avoid all footpaths. He decided to make first for the line of trees along the crest of the high ground, near where he had met Nix repairing Farmer Gorringe's wall, and then cut across country for his destination. This should lessen the risk of any chance encounter with some farmworker returning home to his tea, and of arousing his curiosity.

Brian left by the back door. He passed the ancient dovecot and the site of the old well which Nix had now filled in, and climbed the wall at the end of the orchard. By the time he reached the line of trees the last of the day had faded from the sky. There was plenty of light to see by, however, for not only was the moon shining down between the drifting clouds, but its rays reflected on a sprinkling of snow that had fallen a short while earlier.

On his previous journey in that direction, on the day of going to find Nix, Brian had not taken any special note of the lie of the land. Now he felt that there was no telling how important a thorough knowledge of the local topography might become. As he moved parallel with the wall dividing the trees from the open wold, he glanced this way and that, memorising details.

He saw that the woodland fringe along the crest was very narrow, and that only a few yards beyond the wall the edge of the Cotswold scarp dropped in a steep tree-covered hillside to the low country. Here and there was a gap in the line of timber, exposing a blank of moonlit sky and distance. At one of these, feeling he had plenty of time in hand, Brian slipped over the wall to a point where he could look directly down. The headlights of cars passing along the main road at the base of the descent appeared from that height like moving glow-worms. It made him feel as remote from civilisation as if he had been on the top of Everest.

Brian recrossed the wall and pushed on, taking careful note of each gate in the hedgerows and the easiest spots to clamber over the stone walls. The bulk of Black Knapp loomed nearer, its silvered side humping itself against the night sky. He breasted the lower slopes, and by the time he neared the brow he would have been glad to have been wearing less clothing. He knew, however, that he would probably be thankful for those extra garments before his night's work was over.

He slowed down to a cautious pace as he approached the tumulus on the apex. Though he calculated that he had plenty of time in hand, there was no point in taking chances. As far as he could see, the place was utterly deserted, and, except for the mounds of earth that had been excavated by the archaeologists, it looked as if it had been so since the dawn of history.

As soon as he had made certain that there was nobody about, Brian searched for a suitable spot where he could hide. The difficulty was to guess where those who might be coming were likely to meet. Would it be on one side or the other of the long low mound, or at either of the ends?

He considered whether he should make use of the interior of the ancient tomb, but dismissed the idea as too dangerous. If somebody looked inside with a torch he would be trapped, with no line of retreat to use. A few stunted gorse bushes dotted the top of the hill; he chose a small clump and lay down among them. There, at least, he would not be detected unless he were actually trodden upon.

It did not take him long to cool off after his climb. Though there was no gale as there had been when he was last on the summit of Black Knapp, the light breeze that drifted over the snow-sprinkled crest was icily cold. He felt the warmth disappearing from his body like water trickling from a leaky bucket, and he knew that before long he would be feeling chilled right through. However, he had taken the job on, and would stick it somehow.

Brian drew his hand from beneath him, where he had thrust it for warmth, and glanced at the luminous dial of his wrist-watch. The hands told him that at any time now there was a possibility of someone turning up—that is if anybody were coming at all. He strained his ears to listen for a distant footfall or the rattle of a displaced stone. But the only sounds he heard were those of nature; a flight of wild duck passing on throbbing wings, the plaintive cry of a lapwing as it drifted like a scrap of blown paper over the hill-top, and the occasional querulous hoot of an owl from somewhere down the lower slopes. The only man-made noise which came to him was that of a distant 'plane travelling westwards through the freezing night air.

The soft rustle of something moving through the dry and withered grass to his left brought Brian instantly to the alert, his discomfort forgotten. He peered out between the gorse stems, expecting to see a stealthily approaching figure, the first to reach the rendezvous. But the cause of the sound was only a lone fox which, catching a whiff of Brian's scent, uttered a short bark and took itself off more quickly than it had come.

Once more Brian looked at his watch. It was already well past those two hours after dusk, and if those people were going to show up they should arrive at any moment. At the same time he realised that the betting was strongly in favour of nobody putting in an appearance. Indeed it might be months before any moonlight meeting was again held. Especially considering that Budgeon had been in the area, and might have received verbal orders to pass on to his associates. Still, Brian determined to give them every chance, even if his clothing got frozen to the ground.

The minutes dragged onwards. At last, after waiting a full hour beyond the expected time, he felt certain there could be nothing doing for that night at least. It was not until he started to move that he realised how numbed he was. It cost him a considerable effort to rise to his feet, for his legs had no feeling in them at all. Mechanically he shook the caked snow from the front of his coat, and moved a few tottering steps.

Slowly circulation returned to his limbs as Brian reached the brow and began to descend the slope. By the time he had gained the lower levels the effects of his long cold wait had disappeared, and he was able to stride onward at his normal pace. Taking the same route as that by which he had come, he was soon back at Slad Cottage.

"Well, how did you get on? Did anyone turn up?" exclaimed Frank and Pamela together as they unlocked and opened the door in response to his call.

Brian shook his head. "Might have been at the

North Pole for all the signs of human life," he replied. "It was cold enough for it anyway!"

The following evening Brian again spent a couple of hours lying out on Black Knapp. The weather was still icy, but, oddly enough, knowing what to expect, he felt it less. Once more the result was a negative one, but this time, as he made his way homewards, he had a peculiar feeling that he was not unobserved. Twice he slipped quietly aside after passing a gate and crouched for several minutes behind a hedge to see if anyone were following him, but he could detect no sound or movement whatever.

Nor did the third vigil produce any result. Once more he started to tramp back by the way he had come.

He was nearing the foot of Black Knapp and about to enter the area of fields round its base, when in front of him a figure rose suddenly from behind a low bush. Brian started violently. It instantly flashed through his mind that those for whom he had been lying in wait had turned the tables on him, and meant to put a stop to his curiosity once and for all. He also remembered Copthorne's warning to take to his heels if he were spotted, and not to stop to argue. Brian was about to turn and bolt when he heard a chuckle. "Reckon I scairt you proper!" said a familiar voice. "Same as what you did me a few nights back, time I was settin' one or two snares."

"Oh, it's you, Nix!" exclaimed Brian with relief.

"Ah. 'Oo were you thinkin' I be?"

"Oh, I don't know. It was just seeing you suddenly like that startled me."

Nix gave a disbelieving grin. "Ah! Reckon you're like me now an' agen—been up to summat you didn't ought! What might you ha' been doin' up top o' Black Knapp night-time? It ent the fust, neether—I seen you goin' along two evenin's back."

Brian did some quick thinking. He knew perfectly well that if he gave some futile and improbable reason, such as liking to have a walk by moonlight, that it would only strengthen Nix's curiosity. He would be certain to comment on the subject at the village pub, and within a few hours the whole district would have heard of those nocturnal trips. Brian instinctively realised that the only way to shut Nix's mouth was to tell him the truth; Nix was a sound sort of chap, in spite of his side-slips in the matter of poaching. He need not tell him the whole story, but enough to gain his co-operation. Indeed, his local knowledge might prove exceedingly useful.

"Very possibly you did," replied Brian to Nix's remark. "Now look here, I don't imagine you're the kind of chap to talk if you're asked not to."

"Ah, you're right. More 'arm done by a loose tongue than a loose tooth. What 'a' you been up to?"

"I'll tell you. To begin with, you know Mr. Tilney is in the police?"

"Ah. So I've 'eard tell. Nobody'd never take 'im for a p'lice bloke. 'E's a gent, 'e is."

Brian grinned at the back-hander to the Force. "Well," he went on, "there's some dirty work being done hereabouts, and as Mr. Tilney's laid up, I'm taking his place and trying to find things out." Brian gave a rapid sketch of the situation which had led to Frank's coming to Slad Cottage on leave, omitting, however, any direct mention of the mail-bag robberies, and followed it up with the recognition of Budgeon in the tea-shop and the real reason for Frank's fall into the old well.

"Ah. I reckoned it was a rum-'un 'bout 'im tumblin' in," commented Nix. " 'E knowed well enow it was there."

"Exactly."   Brian continued his tale, speaking of the interview with the detective inspector in Oxford and the incident of the recklessly driven lorry.   He said nothing about having a shrewd idea of which vehicle it was, nor that the death of Romsey—petty thief, copper's nark, and sometime manservant— might not have been in accordance with the verdict at the inquest.   He concluded by recounting how Nix's own tale of figures seen on Black Knapp had led to the idea that the reputedly haunted spot was being used as a meeting-place for rogues.

"Well, blow me if that ent a rum-'un!" was Nix's comment. "So you an' Mr. Tilney reckon what I seen was real folk all the time, not what I thought they was. I wondered why 'e wanted to know, time I was fillin' in that there old well, just when I'd seen 'em, an' 'ow the moon was. If you reckons there's varmints usin' Black Knapp for 'oldin' meetin's an' such, you oughta tell Mr. Goodman on it. 'Tis part of 'is land, an' 'e'd 'elp to chase 'em off."

"Very probably, but you see we don't want them chased off, not until we know who they are, and, with luck, have been able to overhear something of what they go up there to talk about. That's why I've been lying up there the last couple of nights, though nobody's yet turned up," Brian explained. "If he knew, Mr. Goodman might want to charge in and spoil all chance of finding out what we want—like a badly-trained dog at a shooting-party, putting up birds before the guns get within range."

Nix grinned at the simile. "Ah, I wouldn't go for to say you're wrong. 'As a bit of a temper, Mr. Goodman 'as, time 'e's roused. Stan Dawson, what you met t'other day, tell me 'e can be proper awkward when 'e's riled. Not that 'e ent got no complaint of 'im as a master—'e says a nicer gent to work for you wouldn't find."

Nix paused to pull out a charred pipe and set

a light to the dottle of shag it contained. Acrid fumes rose in the frosty air.

"But it's a queer set-up at the mansion," he went on reminiscently.

"In what way?" asked Brian.

"Well, Mr. Goodman 'e live different from the other gentry round about. I mind, time I was a boy, when old Sir John an' 'is fam'ly live at the Manor, there was rare doin's. Carriages three deep bringing guests to parties an' dances an' suchlike. But Goodman 'e don' 'ave no company 'isself, and there ent no servants what we folks want to 'sociate with—that man an' 'is wife what 'e 'as come from Lunnon. Reckon I'm sorry for that Miss Kelly— 'is niece what live there. Fret and worrit she look some'ow, an' ready to jump if she 'ear a pin drop, as the sayin' is. Which go to show livin' in a big 'ouse ent what some folks crack it up to be," Nix ended sententiously.

Brian nodded. He made no spoken comment, however, but reverted to the earlier subject, stressing the need for Nix to say nothing about what he had just been told.

"Ah, you needn't be afeard—I ent got no loose tongue," Nix assured him. "I knows well enow when to say naught."

"I'm sure you do. And it's quite possible later

we may need your help, as you know every inch of these parts."

"Ah. I don' mind givin' an 'and time I'm wanted, though it 'ud be a rum-'un me helpin' the police," said Nix with a grin, remembering some previous dealings with them that were not unconnected with other people's hares and pheasants. "But see 'ere," he added, laying a horny hand on Brian's arm, "there's one thing I ent doin', an' that's layin' up on Black Knapp come night-time. I ent lost no bad luck to go lookin' for it!"

With a laugh Brian assured him that he would not be asked to do so. Then with a nod he continued his homeward journey, leaving Nix to carry on with whatever he had been doing under the silver moon.

As soon as Brian had shed his warm clothing and settled himself before the fire with Frank and Pamela, he spoke of his meeting with Nix and of being compelled by circumstances to tell him about the problem on which they were engaged.

Frank took it badly—no doubt he resented being tied by the leg, or rather the arm, and unable to take any active part. "You'd no right to say anything to Nix," he exploded. "The whole chance of success depends on as few knowing about it as possible. I shouldn't be surprised if you haven't wrecked the whole thing!"

10

"I don't see that at all," replied Brian hotly. He was about to say more when Pamela cut in.

"Of course Brian did the right thing, Frank! I should have thought anybody could see that. If he hadn't taken Nix into his confidence, nothing would have stopped him talking in the pub about seeing Brian on the prowl at night. And anyway, Nix is absolutely trustworthy!"

"He may be—or he may not. Brian had no right——" Frank began.

"Oh shut up!" retorted his sister, and Frank relapsed into disgruntled silence. The atmosphere of tension slowly cleared, but it left Brian with a slight feeling of resentment. After all, Frank was not his boss. He was in this matter with Copthorne's approval, and he considered he had the right to act as circumstances demanded and as he thought fit.

CHAPTER XII

THE LOCKED ROOM

NEXT morning the snow which had been threatening for days was falling heavily.

"I shouldn't think those people of yours, Brian, would be likely to turn up this evening," commented Pamela at breakfast. "The weather will choke them off."

"They may think it an advantage—even less chance of anybody being about," Brian replied. "I shall go up to Black Knapp as usual, having promised Copthorne I would." This reference to the inspector was for Frank's benefit; Brian had not forgotten the little tiff of the night before over the matter of taking Nix into his confidence. "Besides, very possibly the snow will ease up later."

It did, for by noon the snow had ceased to fall, leaving a white layer three inches deep over the countryside.

At lunch Pamela spoke of several things she needed for the house, and Brian volunteered to go down to the village shop to get them. "I'll walk," he went on. "Not that it's too deep on the level for the car, but it may have drifted in places.   I suppose there's nothing very heavy you want brought back?"

"No, only some groceries and sugar.   There's a bag you can take to carry them in—I'll fetch it."

Brian started off down the slad road, his feet crunching crisply in the snow.   The sun had come out, and accompanying him his shadow lay blue across the untrodden surface.

He reached the village street, where the snow no longer retained its virgin whiteness, having been pounded down by both foot-passengers and an occasional van or lorry.   He made his way to the shop and entered.

He handed over the list which Pamela had given him.   The shopkeeper pattered round collecting what was needed, meanwhile keeping up a flow of chatter about the weather.   The bag had just been filled, and Brian was about to turn and leave, when the door behind him opened.   Goodman came in, wearing a shaggy overcoat that made him look like a grizzly bear.

"Hullo, it's you, isn't it, Carter?" he remarked. "I was wondering when I was going to run across you again.   Sorry I was out at the time you and Miss Tilney called—had to attend a cattle sale at Hereford."

Goodman tossed over his order to the man behind the counter, and then spoke again to Brian.

"As I wasn't there you had no chance of seeing that collection of mine—the one I spoke to you and Tilney about the last time we met. What about coming back with me now and having a look at it? My car's outside, and I'll run you up, as I imagine you're walking." Goodman's manner was bluff and hearty.

"It's very kind of you," replied Brian, "but as a matter of fact I ought to be getting straight back. These things I've been getting are wanted at once. Otherwise I'd be very pleased."

"I could send my lad here up with them right away," suggested the shopkeeper. "He's nothing to do at the moment."

"That's right, let him send your stuff," went on Goodman. "It'll give that lazy young feller something to do!" With a laugh and a jerk of his head he indicated the youth who kept his father company behind the counter. "You'll be interested, Carter, in what I've got to show you. Besides," Goodman went on, lowering his voice, "it 'ud do Sybil good— you met my niece, of course, when you were up at the Manor a couple of days ago. It's a lonely life for a gal, for she doesn't see many people. You must stop and have tea with her afterwards. I shall be busy but that needn't hinder, I shall leave Sybil to entertain you."

"Thanks awfully, I'd like to come very much,"

was Brian's answer.　Now that the groceries were to
be sent up he had nothing special to do until nightfall and the time when he must be on his way to
Black Knapp.　He must not fail to keep that
appointment, however, for according to calculations
it was about the last likely night on which anyone
might turn up.　However, if he were given tea
reasonably early, he would have plenty of time to
get back across the fields to the cottage, put on extra
garments, and not be late in arriving on the spot.

"Excellent!" said Goodman.　"Half a minute
while I get what I came for.　There, that's done!
Now come along!"　He moved towards the shop
door.

"One moment!" put in Brian.　"I'd better
scribble a line to send up with the groceries, or
Pamela Tilney will be getting tea ready for me."
He turned towards the shopkeeper who, overhear-
ing, had already produced a pencil from behind his
ear and a piece of paper from beside the till.

"Been asked up to tea at the Manor," wrote Brian
hastily.　"Expect me back about dusk.　If delayed,
will go straight on to the other job."　He initialled
and folded the note.　"You'll send the boy along
with it at once?"

"Ah.　This instant minnit.　Look alive, Bill,
get up along the slad with this 'ere, and them things
for Miss Tilney!"

Brian followed Goodman out, and the big expensive-looking car rolled silently off over the flattened snow. As he drove, Goodman chatted about his hobby and the various things that had been found in the neighbourhood, adding that a number had been found on his property, particularly at the tumulus on the crest of Black Knapp. "Have you been up yet to look at that place?" he asked.

Brian promptly said he had. There was no sense in not doing so, for at the time of his first visit by daylight, in the gale, he had very likely been seen. He had no thought then of escaping observation. But as he replied he could not help wondering if anyone besides Nix knew of his vigils by night. He remembered the odd feeling he had had of being observed when returning on that second occasion. Probably, however, it had been nothing but imagination.

The car drew up before the portico of the big house. Goodman led the way up the steps and ushered Brian inside, and the heavy door closed behind him with a ponderous thud.

The fat and unprepossessing butler appeared from the back regions, and helped his master off with his overcoat. With a face that registered the same look of disapproval that Brian had seen before, he performed a similar office for the guest, and disappeared with both garments to some cloakroom off the main hall.

"The room where I have my things is on the second floor," said Goodman briskly. Brian followed him up the wide stairs with their treads of polished oak, and large and rather dim oil-paintings adorning the walls.

At the sound of their ascent a slim and elfin figure appeared at the top. It was Sybil.

"Brought you a visitor," called Goodman as he caught sight of her. "I've brought Carter along to see my treasures—met him down in the village and ran him up in the car. You know each other, so there's no need to introduce, eh? You'd better come along with us, girl, though you've seen my things before—can't have you getting out of playing hostess. Besides, I've got to go off again soon, and you're going to give our friend tea."

Though there was nothing to which exception could be taken in the words, Brian detected a domineering tone in Goodman's voice. What Pamela had suggested as the cause of Sybil's nervousness at times seemed to be true—Goodman was a bit of a domestic bully, for all his genial-squire-of-the-village manner.

The master of the house turned along a passage, the others following without speaking. He halted before a door and, taking a key from his pocket, unlocked and swung it open. "Here's my museum," he said to Brian. "Come along and have a look at it."

The room was of a fair size and well lighted by large windows looking out on to the garden at the back. Its walls were panelled in oak that had not been altered like the front of the house, but dated from the original building. Though the room was by no means fitted up as a study, in one corner stood a large desk. The main features, however, were a couple of long tables across the middle, bearing glass-topped show-cases. Goodman crossed towards them and lifted the cover of the nearest.

He certainly knew how to make things interesting. Brian found himself becoming quite absorbed in those various relics of the past, the primitive ornaments and weapons and domestic utensils of pre-historic man. Each was neatly labelled with the place and date of discovery, and it amazed him that so much had come to light in the comparatively small area round Kinford. He found himself asking questions about the probable use of sundry strange objects, and receiving answers that were both clear and concise.

With Brian beside him, Goodman moved along the line of exhibits, while Sybil followed mutely a yard behind. At length the inspection was completed, and Goodman glanced at his watch. Brian did the same, and was surprised to see how much time had slipped by, for it was already close on four o'clock.

"I must leave you now—I've other things to do," said Goodman. He waved them out of the door, and paused to turn and pocket the key. Brian wondered why he was so particular about relocking the room—no burglar would be likely to want to pinch the kind of stuff it contained. Having thrown a curt order to Sybil to take the visitor up to her quarters and give him tea, Goodman strode off without waiting for Brian's thanks for the trouble he had taken.

Left together, Brian glanced at the girl. She smiled and led the way along the passage and up another flight of stairs to the floor above.

As Brian had anticipated from Pamela's description, the room into which he was ushered was small and not very attractive. Indeed, in the days when there had been a large staff in the house, it had probably been one of the servants' bedrooms. Like the museum, it looked out over the snow-covered garden far below.

Sybil seemed at ease as soon as she had entered it. Obviously she felt far more at home in her own little sitting-room than anywhere else in the big house. Tea had already been placed on the table in the centre. As the day was beginning to fade, Sybil switched on the light, for unlike Slad Cottage, the Manor was on the grid.   She silently motioned to Brian to take a seat.

While she poured out, Brian started to make conversation, but found his efforts falling somewhat flat. Sybil answered only in monosyllables.   Switching from things like the weather and what he had been shown by Goodman, Brian began to speak of his life in London, of shows he had recently seen, and of various amusing incidents he had come across.   His efforts, however, had a different result from what he intended.   To his surprise he saw tears appearing in her violet eyes.

"I say, what's the matter?" he could not help exclaiming.

For answer the girl turned her face away, and to Brian's discomfort he saw her shoulders give a convulsive shake and heard a stifled sob.

A moment later Sybil recovered herself and once more turned to face him.   "Frightfully sorry!" she murmured, "but what you've just been saying brought back memories.   I used to know once what it was to have a good time, but now——"

"Look here," said Brian bluntly.   "What's the trouble?   Why not tell me about it?   Nothing like getting things off your chest, as they say."

"Well——"   Sybil smiled wanly.   "It would be a relief to talk about it.   Would you mind?"

"Of course not. Fire away! I promise not to repeat anything you tell me."

Thus encouraged, Sybil went on. "It's the kind of life I lead here, never getting a chance of going anywhere or seeing anybody, and nobody of the kind who would interest me coming to the house. It was all so different when my parents were alive—they were returning from a visit to Ireland two years ago when the ship went down; you may remember the disaster." It was put in a confusing way, but Brian saw what she meant. "Uncle came at once when he heard the news and was most kind; he was my only near relation and insisted I should come to the Manor. I'd stayed here before, and liked it, so I eagerly accepted. I didn't realise then what it would become," she ended with a gesture of her small hands.

"Your uncle bullies you, doesn't he?" remarked Brian. "I noticed the way he spoke to you just now."

"Oh no, I wouldn't call it that," replied Sybil in a voice that carried no conviction. "At first he was nice enough to me, though now I feel that he wishes he had not been so ready to do what I expect he considered his duty. It's been worse recently. Perhaps something's gone wrong with his affairs, though I know nothing about them."

Sybil paused, and Brian waited for her to go on.

"Then there's Symonds, the butler you know. He's always following me with his eyes as I move about the house, as if he suspected me of wanting to steal the spoons."

"Perhaps he wants to make sure that nobody sees *him* doing so," commented Brian. "He looks a thoroughly nasty bit o' work!"

"I know, and his wife is nearly as bad. So between all that, and never getting any fun, I sometimes have a feeling I'm living in a sort of madhouse, with very possibly a corpse concealed under the dining-room table!" She laughed hysterically.

"Steady!" said Brian. "Getting all het up won't do any good. I should have thought the answer to all this was fairly simple. If you can't stick things here, get a job."

"How could I? I've had no training in anything."

"There's that, of course," Brian admitted. "On the other hand there must be lots of girls in the same boat these days, and they get away with it. When I go back to work I'll make enquiries and let you know if I hear of anything suitable. You could then come up to Town for an interview."

"That's all very well, but I've no money. It's all in trust somewhere and Uncle doles it out by pennies. He'd never put up the fare."

"Then hitch-hike, dash it! Unless you're afraid

of offending your uncle," Brian could not help adding, for to his optimistic outlook Sybil seemed to be suggesting needless difficulties.

"I hate him!" said Sybil violently. "No, I didn't really mean that, but——"

"Well, think it over. We'll have another talk soon." Brian glanced at his watch, and realised it was already past the time he had intended to leave. He rose quickly to his feet. "I must be off," he said. "Thanks for the tea."

"And thanks ever so much for what you've said and done—listening to me like that," responded Sybil. "It's cheered me up no end, discussing things with you."

"That's all right. Keep your chin up. 'Be seein' you'." He moved towards the door.

He turned the handle, but the door did not move. He tried again, giving a harder tug. It still refused to open. "What the deuce is the matter with it?" Brian muttered. After a few more tugs he realised that the door was not stuck but locked.

How had it happened? Brian asked himself. There had been no indication of anything wrong with the door when he and Sybil had entered. Had someone sneaked up quietly while they were talking, and silently turned the key on the outside? And if so, who? That sinister butler, who looked so disapproving on arrival, had he anything to do with it? And for what reason?

Meanwhile Sybil had come forward. "Oh dear!" she exclaimed. "I suppose the lock must have slipped somehow into its socket. We shall have to wait till someone comes to let us out."

'If we gave a good shout together, wouldn't your uncle hear us and come along?"

"Uncle's gone out."

"You're sure?"

"Yes, he told me so. You remember he said he'd something else to do, though I don't know what."

"That fat butler and his wife might hear us if we yelled," suggested Brian.

"They wouldn't . They live in the lower rooms, miles away. We'll just have to wait, I'm afraid, till Uncle comes back. It'll only mean you'll be home later—you're in no hurry, are you?"

"On the contrary, I am!" Brian ejaculated. The urgent need of getting to Black Knapp now filled his mind, especially as this was probably the last likely evening for any meeting there. "I've an urgent appointment to keep," he went on. "Never mind what it is, but it's vital."

He turned again towards the door, wondering whether there was any connexion between it and his watching job. He flung his weight against it, but the door might have been a stone wall for all the effect it had, being constructed of solid oak a couple of inches thick.

"Oh, you'll hurt yourself!" cried Sybil as he recoiled from the immovable barrier.

"I've done that already," Brian replied with a wry grin, rubbing his shoulder. "No getting out that way, I'm afraid, so it's a case of having to think up something else."

CHAPTER XIII

THE MEETING IN THE SNOW

BRIAN moved from the door and crossed over quickly to the window.

He thrust out his head. Daylight had disappeared some time before, but the rays of the rising full-moon, slanting across the snow and reflecting from it, made things clearly visible.

Brian had forgotten how far up he was, and the flights of stairs he had ascended since entering the Manor. The window was nearly forty feet above the paved stone footpath that divided the wall of the house from the lawns. Dropping from the sill was out of the question—it would only result in being killed or badly injured, and that would not help the situation at all.

He withdrew his head and took a quick glance round the room. Had it contained a bed he had an idea that sheets and blankets could be tied together by the corners to serve as a rope, but there was nothing which could be used in that way. Even the window curtains were plastic and of no size at all. Once more he leaned out over the sill, looking this way and that, and taking no notice of Sybil's agitated remarks.

A couple of yards to his left Brian saw a black line of shadow, cast by a down-pipe for rainwater, bisecting the moon-silvered wall. He twisted his neck and looked upwards. The eaves of the house roof were close overhead, the line of guttering passing just above the window.

If the pipe had been within reach he saw it would be a simple matter to lower himself down it, but those two yards of distance might have been as many miles for all the use he could make of it. To stand on the sill and jump in the hope of grasping it would be as good as deliberate suicide; he would never be able to clutch it and at the same time check his falling weight. Once more he looked upwards.

That guttering—could it be used as a bridge by which to reach the down-pipe? It struck him as a pretty desperate idea, but it seemed the only alternative to staying where he was and giving up all hope of reaching Black Knapp within the time limit.

Cautiously he got his knees on to the sill, steadying himself by holding on to the edge of the open window. Sybil gave a low cry of alarm. "I'll be all right," Brian replied, trying to keep a steadiness in his voice which he did not feel. "I'll manage, so don't you worry. Sorry to leave so unceremoniously.

Say good-bye to your uncle for me," he added, with
an attempt at a grin.

He rose to his feet.   Now came the difficult part,
that of standing upright and letting go of the window in order to reach upwards for the edge of the
guttering.   Was it firmly fixed, or would it give way
under his weight and send him crashing down on to
those snow-covered flags below?

He grasped it, hooking his fingers inside the rough
lip.   It seemed to be securely fastened.   It was now
or never—he dared not linger lest his nerve should
give way.   He took his feet off the sill.

Hanging by his hands, and with his legs dangling
in space, he inched his way along.   The strain on
his arms seemed intolerable, but there could be no
going back now.   After what seemed an age he felt
his side touch the down-pipe.   He released one hand
and grasped it.   In getting the other hand round it
he nearly fell, and was saved only by the grip he had
now obtained with his knees, which took off some of
the weight.   With a gasp of relief Brian realised
that the worst was over; lowering himself down the
pipe was nothing to what had gone before.

His feet reached solid ground.   For a moment he
stood motionless, experiencing the joy of letting the
muscles of his arms relax.   Then he glanced upwards, waved to Sybil whose head he could see

projecting anxiously from the window high above, and turned to go.

He realised that the shortest way to Black Knapp was across the lawns and through the belt of trees between them and the cowsheds. He had little fear of finding himself held up by a spiked boundary-fence to the garden, or an impenetrable hedge, for there was sure to be a gate giving access from the garden to the farmyard. Sure enough, as he passed beneath the trees with their black branches outlined in white against the dark sky, he reached a small gate set in a high wall.

Beyond it, he found himself at the back of the cowsheds. Except for the occasional lowing of a beast no sound came from them, for Dawson and his mates had long since knocked off and gone home. Brian hurried past them, across the snow that had been trodden up by the boots of the men going to and fro with feeding-stuffs. The cold was fierce, and he thought ruefully of his overcoat which still hung in the Manor cloakroom where the fat butler had put it. But there was no time now to fetch another from Slad Cottage. He must just do without one, and hope that the exercise would warm him up.

He hastened onwards at a shuffling run, scrambling over loose-stone walls and vaulting gates in the intervening hedgerows. He could see no other footprints on the layer of snow that covered the fields; if the men had already gone to Black Knapp they must have approached it by a different route.   It occurred to Brian that a fall of snow might have caused some alteration in their plans.   They would surely realise that tracks would be left.   But perhaps it had come too late to postpone the prearranged plan.

The steep side of the wold rose before him, and as he breasted it he slackened his pace.   It would never do to reach the brow out of breath, lest his panting should be heard by those whom he might find on the crest.   He wished he had something white to wrap round him, for it struck him that he would be visible at a considerable distance against the moonlit snow.   However, if anybody were up there they would probably be equally visible to him, and he must just make sure of spotting them first and dropping somewhere out of sight.

Brian reached the brow and the edge of the more level ground on the top.   Crouching, and ready to drop flat in an instant, he moved cautiously forward. He could see the long low mound of the tumulus quite distinctly, but no figures were visible beside it.   Was he early in arriving after all, or were his efforts to result in another blank night like his previous vigils?

He was taking no chances, however.   Making use

of the cover afforded by the stunted gorse bushes
which dotted the crest, he crept onwards towards the
prehistoric mound.　He reached the spot where he
had hidden those last three times, and lay down.　It
was the best place available, and he would once more
wait there to see if anything happened.

He had hardly wriggled himself beneath the snow-
laden stems of the gorse when he heard distinctly
the sound of voices.　Yet he could see no sign of
anyone.　Where on earth could those voices come
from?　Surely not from inside that low dark burial-
chamber?　Suddenly he tumbled to the situation;
those whose voices he could hear were on the far
side of the tumulus and hidden from him by its
rounded bulk.

Brian's heart leaped.　Things could not have
worked out better!　He had only to approach and
climb the mound to be able to look directly down on
those who were behind it.　Silently he rose from his
hiding-place and made his way forward.

On hands and knees he ascended, and then lying
prone he wriggled himself forward on his chest.　He
could make out the figures now—there were four of
them, standing just at the base of the further side.
He flattened himself into the snow, keeping his head
down lest it should be seen against the skyline, and
peered at those below him.

The man nearest to him was Budgeon—there was

no mistaking that dangling lock of hair drooping over his hatless forehead. Two of the others were strangers to him; but the fourth, the man who was doing the talking, was familiar enough—there was no mistaking Brian's late host at the Manor.

Brian felt a surge of disappointment. There seemed no doubt that Goodman had also got wind of persons seen on Black Knapp, and was telling them off for trespassing on his property. That meant the meeting would be broken up before it had really started, and with it all chance of finding out any of the things which Inspector Copthorne wanted to know.

At the same time it struck Brian that Goodman's voice did not sound like that of an angry landowner choking off trespassers; it continued in an even flow rather than in abrupt sentences. Brian concentrated on listening, and found that he could hear quite plainly.

"Now I had better explain in greater detail," Goodman was saying. "As I told you, the Bank will be sending this big consignment of one-pound notes to the Vernon Street Post Office next Friday about noon, in time to catch the early afternoon's registered mail. When does your informant say that the mail-van leaves, Budgeon?"

"Two-thirty prompt."

"Very well, then. At two-twenty-eight on the

tick," Goodman went on, addressing one of those whom Brian did not know, "you, Walters, will pinch a car from the car-park in Lower Place. This will prevent trouble if anyone spots the number later. Halt it opposite the Toft Street Post Office not later than two-thirty-three. The van is due to pick up more mail there at two-thirty-five, before going on to the G.P.O. You'll have two men loafing on the pavement—choose them well and see they're reliable. It's their job to cosh the van-driver, chuck the registered mail into your waiting car, and disappear. You will then drive off at full speed to the quiet back-street behind the George Hotel . . ."

Brian's brain, as he listened, was in a whirl. He could hardly believe his ears. Yet there was no doubt about it whatever. Goodman, the landowner, J.P., and highly successful breeder of pedigree stock, was none other than the master-planner whom the police had sought for so long. Behind that extremely respectable camouflage lay Goodman's really paying line of business!

Brian's mind flashed back to past events, and one by one they fell into place in the light of what he now knew. There had been Frank's "accident"; had not Goodman inspected the old well? No doubt he had told Budgeon about it in case the knowledge might come in useful—as it had when Budgeon found himself followed at the time he, presumably, was on his way to keep an appointment with Goodman at or near the Manor. Then that day Brian and Pamela had gone to Oxford. They had met Goodman just after they had started, and Pamela had told him about an appointment. That, immediately after Frank's "accident", must have roused Goodman's suspicions. No doubt he had gone straight back to the Manor and arranged by 'phone to have them "tailed" on arrival. Copthorne had met them at the door of the house, been recognised, and information transmitted back to Goodman. It seemed a likely supposition.

Then again, that lorry incident. Brian had been right in recognising that vehicle in the yard at the Manor, but it had never occurred to him that its owner had arranged for it to be "taken without permission" from the spot where Dawson had left it. He ought to have thought of that, Brian ruminated; after all, who else would have known that Dawson was off work that day and where the lorry had been parked? And who had been in the driving cab? Probably those two strangers now listening to what Goodman was saying.

And lastly, the events of that very afternoon. Goodman had known of Brian's vigils on Black Knapp, and his invitation to the Manor, and what followed had been planned to prevent him being there on the date fixed for the meeting. It must have been Goodman and not the unattractive butler who had silently locked the door of Sybil's room, and no doubt he still imagined he had succeeded in his object.

Brian smiled at the thought. He smiled also at his recollection of having suggested to Frank that Goodman's co-operation, as the owner of Black Knapp, should be enlisted. That would have put the complete lid on any hope of finding out anything!

All these things flashed through Brian's head in a matter of a few seconds, and made no interruption in his listening to what Goodman was saying. Every word that he could remember would be of value to Copthorne, together with the appearance of the two men whom he did not know.

Goodman was now speaking to his third companion.

"At two-thirty-six, Milton, you will be cruising slowly down that street—with plenty of dirt rubbed on the number-plates, by the way. Walters will come up alongside. Transfer the bag and buzz off, taking Walters with you and abandoning Walters' stolen car."

"Having got the goods, where do I take 'em?" asked Milton. "Same place as before?"

Goodman snorted. "You know me well enough

to be aware it's never the same place! Do you know
Bolter's Timber Yard?"

"Can't say I do, but I can find out before Friday."

"Make sure you do, then. I'll be there, just beyond the main entrance, at two-forty. I'll take
charge of the loot, and you and Walters can then
clear off. Mind you clean the number-plates at
once, or you'll have some 'flattie' holding you up for
having them obscured. Is that all understood?"

There was a general murmur of assent. Then
Budgeon asked, "When is the share-out to be?"

"In a day or two. The usual percentage, plus
something extra for the men you employ as helpers.
I'll arrange all that later, though."

Brian realised that the meeting was ending. He
had heard a good deal, but owing to his late arrival
he had missed all the opening part of the discussion
and had no clue as to where the robbery being
planned was to take place. It might be in London
or any large city. Still, the street-names and so on
would help, and no doubt Copthorne could puzzle
out the exact scene of operations from them. In the
meantime Brian saw he must concentrate on the
immediate present; he had better remain motionless
until the party dispersed before attempting to make
his own getaway.

Unfortunately the man called Walters happened
to turn and look towards the long hump of the

tumulus.   He caught sight of the small blob on the top that was Brian's head.   He made a step forward, peered intently, and gave an exclamation.

The others spun round as one man.   "A snooper!" cried Budgeon, and started to scramble up the mound, with Milton close at his heels.

There was not an instant to lose.   Brian sprang to his feet, dashed down the farther side, and sprinted across the level top of Black Knapp towards the brow of the descent.   As he plunged over it he heard the angry voices and pounding feet of those who pursued.

As he sprinted down the slope, Brian remembered Romsey—the man with a shady reputation whose body he had found in the road on the day of his arrival at Kinford.   Had *he* got hold of something too, hoping to get a reward for informing the police? It flashed through Brian's mind that there might be an inquest on himself shortly if he failed to out-distance those behind; they would not repeat the "road accident", being too smart to do the same thing twice, but there are plenty of places where a body can be convincingly dumped!

Having had no overcoat to protect him, Brian had become decidedly chilled while waiting and listen-ing on the top of the mound, but now he was thank-ful he was not burdened with extra clothing.   He hoped sincerely that those behind were not in good training, and would soon become blown and give up. If he could lengthen the distance between himself and his pursuers he would be able to dodge and throw them off his trail, though this was not possible until he was on the more level ground with its hedges and stone walls.

Stumbling more than once, for there were unseen snags hidden under the layer of snow, Brian came to the first wall. He vaulted over it, and doubled. A shout from behind told him that this had been seen. Over the next gate he went, and jinked again.

The course he was forced to take was in almost the opposite direction to Slad Cottage. This could not be helped, however. He must keep on going until he had shaken off the enemy, and then find his way home by a roundabout route. It might take some time, but anything was better than being caught—he could guess only too well what the result of that would be!

Twice Brian paused for a moment to listen. The second time he could hear no sound of pursuit. The moonlit silence of the night was unbroken, and it seemed fairly certain that the chase had been abandoned. He wondered if he had been recognised, but felt pretty positive he had not. Though Goodman would learn in time about his escape from Sybil's locked room, he would have no proof that the watcher on Black Knapp was not somebody quite different.

He hurried onwards over the snow, knowing that he had a long tramp ahead of him before he could reach Slad Cottage, report to Frank, and get busy with the telephone.

CHAPTER XIV

AFTER THE MEETING

BRIAN was mistaken in his idea that he had not been recognised.

The men who had been chasing him returned to the foot of Black Knapp, where they found Goodman waiting for them. "Did you catch him?" was the first thing he asked.

The others shook their heads. "The blighter got away from us," they admitted.

Goodman swore. "What sort of chap was he?" he continued. "Some village yokel?"

It was Budgeon who replied. "Oh, I spotted the beggar all right. Him an' me has met before. It was that young chap I told you about last time I was down here—him what I saw with that police spy Tilney, when I was havin' a cuppa tea in a caff. Him what follered me along o' Tilney the night I gave that copper bloke what-for by pushin' him into that pit."

"You mean Carter? Man, that's impossible! At the present moment I've got him shut up securely in a top-floor room at the Manor, and he'll be stoppin' there till I choose to go and let him out. Pity you can't use your eyes better!"

"Sez you!" retorted Budgeon, his annoyance getting the better of his respect for his boss. "All I can say is, guv'nor, you must ha' locked up the wrong bloke!"

"That's rubbish—I know Carter well enough."

"Well, it was him all right," replied Budgeon with a shrug. "And now he's got away, I suppose he'll go an' blow the gaff on us. Gonnows how long he was listenin'-in to what you was tellin' us. I guess this has mucked things up proper; I've had a spell in the cooler before, and I ain't lookin' for another."

Once more Goodman swore feelingly. He still could not believe that the intruder had been Brian, although Budgeon seemed so positive. It was impossible that he should have got out, and yet the impossible sometimes did happen.

"Supposing you're right," Goodman went on. "It strikes me those two, Tilney and Carter, are going to upset our apple-cart if we don't take steps to prevent it." He turned angrily towards his lieutenants. "Why the blazes couldn't you chaps have done things properly when you had the chance, instead of bungling things? Why couldn't you, Budgeon, have made sure that Tilney broke his neck instead of his arm when you pushed him into that old well? And you, Walters, you went and botched the job of run-

ning down Carter and the girl as they were coming
back from Oxford, though I told you where to get
the lorry, and the time and place to be looking out
for them on the road. Am I the only one who's able
to do things properly? When I caught that coppers'
nark Romsey getting through the window of my
study at two o'clock in the morning, hoping to get
some evidence he could sell to the police, didn't I
knock him on the head, get my car out, and dump
him before daylight in that little-used road near
where he worked at Lethwick's, after bumping over
him to leave tyre-marks and make things look
natural?"

"O.K., guv'nor, O.K.!" came the retort as soon as
Goodman stopped for breath. "But all that ain't
gettin' us no further with Carter. You ain't been
so blinkin' clever there—you says you had him
locked up where he couldn't get out, but he didn't
stay put! So what?"

"I shall take steps to settle his hash once and for
all. And Tilney's, too, and the girl's, if it comes to
that," replied Goodman, mastering his temper and
speaking more calmly.

"That's all very well, but it ain't in the bargain
to finish up on a murder charge," put in Milton, who
had not so far spoken.

"There'll be no fear of that if you do what I tell
you!" Goodman snapped back. "I've never let you

12

chaps down so far, and I shan't now.   The first thing to do is to stop Carter using the telephone when he gets back to where he is staying."

"You mean by cuttin' the wires?"

"No, only a fool would do that, leaving them hanging for the police to find and know they'd been tampered with.   What's needed is for someone to scramble up a pole and short-circuit the lines with a bit of wire, which can be removed before morning without leaving a trace.   The quicker it's done the better.   You know the ground best, Budgeon.   Off you go and do it!"

"I ain't got no wire," Budgeon protested.

"Find some then!   Look here, the shortest way from here to that cottage is past the Manor.   You'll find some knocking about near the cowsheds.   Meanwhile Walters and Milton and I will go on to the house—I don't like any of you being seen there, but it won't matter for once and I'm not going to hang about here in the cold.   In the meanwhile I'll tell them my plans.   Rejoin us, Budgeon, when you've fixed that 'phone, and we'll then prepare for the next part of the night's work."

When Budgeon had gone off, Goodman turned to his other accomplices.   He had now fully regained his temper and spoke slowly and calmly.

"It's quite simple really.   There must be another sad accident which will be completely effective this time. On a cold night like this—and it *is* cold, you know—people are liable to stoke up their fires and leave them burning after they go to bed. A beam in the chimney may catch alight—Slad Cottage is an old building, you know—or hot coals may roll out on to the hearth-rug, and before anyone sleeping there woke, the whole place might be a raging inferno."

"Stow it, guv'nor, and come down to brass tacks," commented Milton. "What's the game?"

"I'll put it more clearly," Goodman replied. "In an hour or two's time we'll all take a stroll down to Slad Cottage and see if there's any light in the windows. If there isn't, we'll conclude they've all gone to bed. Then we'll enter silently, slip upstairs and knock 'em all on the head, and set the place alight. It's some distance from the village and nobody's likely to be awake there; by the time the flames are seen and the fire brigade called, there'll be nothing left of the building but the outer stone walls, for the floors and rafters will burn like tinder and the bodies will be only charred remains buried among the ashes and the tiles of the collapsed roof. Simple, eh?"

"Dead easy!" retorted Milton tersely. "We'd be all ends up if it didn't come off. Besides, how are we goin' to get in? Bustin' down the door will wake 'em, and like as not they'll hop it out o' the back or somewhere."

Goodman smiled. "At the Manor I have an excellent key which I'll take with me. Some time ago, when everybody was out, and I'd seen the woman who works there leave, I had a look round inside, and made myself familiar with the lay-out. She'd left the door key conveniently under a stone, as these women do. When leaving I took an impression of that key before putting it back. It was easy then to have a duplicate cut."

"You're a marvel, guv'nor!" put in Walters admiringly. "You thinks of everything."

"Naturally. Those who don't think get caught. That should reassure you, Milton," he added, turning to the one who had raised objections. "And now let's go along to the Manor, and wait there till Budgeon comes back. We could do with a drink or two to warm us up. Besides, I want to find out how Carter got away—if he did do so, that is."

When he had settled his companions with a bottle and glasses in front of them, Goodman climbed the stairs to Sybil's room. He turned the key in the lock and entered. The girl started up from the chair in which she had been sitting.

"Where's Carter?" he demanded, as soon as a glance round the room told him that she was alone.

"He—we found the door locked—he wanted to

go, but couldn't," Sybil replied, shrinking back at the sight of Goodman's angry expression. "So he climbed out of the window and left that way—he said he had an appointment to keep and couldn't wait till somebody came to let us out."

"Impossible! That's a lie!" Goodman crossed the room in a couple of strides and looked out at the moonlit landscape. "It's a forty-foot drop! Come on, how did he manage to get away?"

"I've told you, Uncle. We were locked in, and——"

"*I* locked you both in, and for a good enough reason. Well, how is it that he isn't here now?"

"He said he must get away somehow. He reached out of the window for the guttering above, and clawed his way along to the down-pipe and from there to the ground."

"And you helped him, eh?" Goodman snarled, for a second glance through the window had shown him Brian's footprints in the snow.

"Oh no, I was terrified he'd fall, and begged him not to try. But he would do it. He got to the bottom safely, and hurried off across the garden. That was the last I saw of him."

"That's the last you'll ever see of him! I've had enough annoyance from him, and that fellow Tilney and his sister, too, if it comes to that. By morning the lot of 'em 'll be nothing but charred corpses!"

"But . . . Uncle, what do you mean?   You can't know what you're saying!"

"I know very well what I'm saying, and what I'm doing, too!"   In his annoyance at the unsatisfactory turn which events had taken that evening, he began to speak recklessly, feeling that he had his niece under his thumb and that she would never dare to give him away.   "How do you think I make the money to afford to live in a place like this, keep a big car and subscribe to every silly local charity, besides keeping a big balance at the bank?   Out of pedigree cattle?"

Sybil made no reply.   She had not seen her uncle before in this violent mood, and was scared.

"Bah!   That business hardly covers expenses. I've got a proposition that's a good deal better pay-ing!"   In two or three sentences Goodman told her of his long-standing success in organising robberies. "And that boy friend of yours you had to tea," he went on, "he and Tilney have been shoving their noses in where they aren't wanted.   I and my men —there are two down below at this moment, and three if the other's come back—are going down to Slad Cottage presently to lay 'em out and set the place alight!   Accidental fires are common in winter-time, and that's what everybody 'll think it was.   I don't make mistakes, any more than I did when I settled Romsey's hash for him!"

Sybil remained silent, staring at her uncle with eyes wide with horror.

"Yes, Romsey, that pompous fool Lethwick's manservant! He thought he could pull a fast one on me, but he soon found out differently. As your friends at Slad Cottage are shortly going to discover—I'm not the man to allow my plans to be upset!"

Goodman turned on his heel and went out, slamming the door violently behind him. For several minutes after the echoes had died away Sybil did not move, amazement and horror chasing each other through her brain. As she had told Brian, she had recently grown to dislike her uncle, but she had never suspected—this! She gave herself a shake as if to throw off the shock of the recent interview, and turned her mind to thinking of some way of warning Brian what was afoot.

Even though he knew he had some distance to go, Brian had not realised how far he had been chased in the wrong direction before shaking off his pursuers. At last, however, he found himself on familiar ground, and saw the lights of the cottage gleaming ahead.

In response to his call Pamela let him in. She cried out when she saw the state of his clothes, which bore traces of the snow he had crawled in and had collected several tears during his flight. "What have you been doing?" she exclaimed.

"Let me get to the fire and I'll tell you," replied Brian. He entered the sitting-room. Frank looked up, laying down the book he was reading. Brian took his stand with his back to the hearth, and announced: "I've succeeded at last. I know the man whom you've been looking for for so long, and I've been listening to him giving instructions to Budgeon and Co. I've collected a packet of evidence—plenty for Copthorne to get busy on and make a move."

Frank and Pamela looked up eagerly. "Who is it?" they asked together.

"Goodman."

The name might have been a bomb for the effect it produced on Brian's companions.

"You're crazy!" ejaculated Frank. "Goodman's the last possible person! Either you're drunk or gone off your rocker!"

Brian laughed. "You said yourself that it was probably the most unlikely man in the world, and you were right. Our highly respected squire of the Manor is the lad you police chaps have been seeking all this time."

"But I say, look here——"

Brian checked Frank's outburst with a gesture. "Listen, both of you, while I tell you exactly what happened since I sent you up that note with the groceries, telling you I'd been asked up to tea at the Manor."

Keeping to essential facts, Brian described his adventures. From seeing the collection he went on to speak of his talk with Sybil at tea, and the discovery that they had been locked in. He went on to tell of his perilous escape by the window and his hurried journey across the snow in the hope of reaching Black Knapp before the breaking-up of any possible meeting that might be taking place there. He recounted his initial surprise at seeing Goodman, and his first idea that he was warning off trespassers. He went on to repeat what he had heard Goodman saying, thus proving beyond a doubt that he was the head of the whole business, and ended up with the tale of the way he had been chased by Budgeon and the other two men, and how he had managed to get clear away.

His hearers were dumbfounded as they realised what it all implied.

"Then Lethwick doesn't come into the picture at all?" Frank commented at length.

"Not as far as I know. We were barking up the wrong tree there, I imagine."

"Were you recognised when they chased you?" asked Pamela.

"I may have been, but I don't think so. In the

meantime we'd better get cracking. The first thing to do is to ring up Inspector Copthorne and let him know all about this." Without waiting for Frank's agreement, Brian crossed over to the telephone.

"What's the matter? Can't you get anybody?" said Frank presently from his chair.

"No. The thing seems completely dead."

"Then you *were* recognised, and Goodman has made the first move. Sent someone along to cut the wires, I expect, between here and the village."

Brian gave a grunt of annoyance. He was tired, and longed to stretch himself in a chair and take it easy after all his exertions. "That means, I suppose, that I'll have to go down to the call-box in the village and ring through from there." He felt in his pockets to see if he had the money for the coin-box. "I'll borrow your overcoat, Frank—mine's still reposing at the Manor. I'll run down in the car," he added. "Quicker that way. Besides, if the blighter who's put the 'phone out of action is waiting for me on the road, he'll get run over if he tries to stop me!"

Brian put on the borrowed overcoat, picked up a torch, and went out to the shed at the back. He opened the double doors wide and hooked them in position. He got into the driving-seat of his car and pressed the self-starter. It buzzed merrily, but the engine did not fire.

"Cold!" he muttered. "I ought to have had a radiator lamp." Brian tried again, with no better luck.

He got out, withdrew the starting-handle from under the back seat, and swung the engine by hand. Still there was no response. He tried the starter again—same result.

"There's plenty of petrol," he muttered. "Perhaps the plugs are damp or something." He lifted the side of the bonnet and flashed his torch inside. It did not take him long to find what the trouble was. The cap of the distributor hung loose on its wires, and the rotor was missing.

He dropped the bonnet with a clang and turned to Frank's car which stood alongside. Before attempting to start it he opened the flap and shone his torch on the engine. It had been immobilised in the same way.

Budgeon had done his work well. After short-circuiting the telephone he had remembered the cars, and before rejoining Goodman and the others had slipped silently round to the back of Slad Cottage and made sure of them being useless.

Brian went back to the house and reported what he had found. "There's no help for it," he said, "I shall have to go on foot. I'll be as quick as I can."

"Have something hot to drink first," said Pamela,

appearing with a cup and a steaming jug in her hand. "I've just got it ready for you."

"Thanks. Very thoughtful of you," Brian replied absently, his mind on other things. "And then I must be off."

He had just emptied the cup and was setting it down when all three heard a gentle but urgent rapping on the outer door. Instinctively they looked at each other, wondering who it could be. The rapping came again, and Pamela made a move. Brian gently pushed past her, after picking up the poker from the fireplace—there was no knowing who might be outside.

Brian opened the door. He would not have been surprised to see some sinister figure covering him with a pistol. To his amazement he found Sybil on the doorstep. She wore no coat, and only thin slippers were on her feet—hardly the best equipment in which to be out in the cold and snow.

CHAPTER XV

THROUGH THE DARK WOODS

"OH, I say! What on earth's brought——?" began Brian. He broke off as Pamela pushed past him and drew the girl inside.

"Come to the fire and get warm," she said. "You must be frozen."

"N-no. I ran all the way." Sybil blinked as she stepped into the lamplight. "I've come to warn you all," she went on hurriedly. "I've found out what sort of a man Uncle really is, and it's all too horrible. And he's planning to do dreadful things to-night!"

"Take it easy," said Pamela soothingly, gently pushing the girl into a chair in front of the hearth. "That's better. Have something warming to drink, and then you can tell us what's brought you here."

There was still some hot liquid in the jug from which Brian had filled his cup, and as Sybil drank, it had a steadying effect on her. The colour returned to her face, and when she spoke again it was in a quieter and less frightened tone.

"Listen!" she began, turning to Brian and addressing him rather than the others. "After you got away

I waited and waited in my locked room.   At last I heard the key turn and Uncle came in.

"He was very angry, and accused me of helping you to get away.   He said he'd locked us in intentionally, and then went on to tell me the most frightful things—things I'd never had the slightest suspicion of before.   About the way he's been making his money.   He even admitted to having done a murder—that man Romsey, you know—and then faked it to look like an accident."

She paused, looking from one to the other as if she expected to be told that she was imagining it all. The unruffled expressions on the faces of her hearers surprised her.

"I'm afraid we've found out already that your uncle isn't the shining light he pretends to be," said Brian quietly.

"You know about him?   But how?"

"For some time we've suspected that there was an unknown person living in this neighbourhood who was running an organised crime syndicate, though it was only this evening, to our great surprise I may add, that I obtained proof that your uncle was the man."   Brian added a brief account of his recent adventures.

"But I haven't told you all!"   Sybil glanced over her shoulder as if expecting to see danger at her elbow.   "He's planning to stop you ever reporting to the police. He said he had three men with him, and the four of them are going to come down here as soon as they think you are all in bed, and kill you and set fire to the house to cover the traces of their crime! You must all get away quickly, or else get the police here at once. There's no time to be lost!"

"So that's the game, is it?" said Brian with a coolness that he did not feel. "A nice little visiting party of four—Messrs. Budgeon, Walters and Milton under the leadership of your respected uncle. You've done wonderfully, bringing us warning. Don't worry, we'll upset their plan somehow. By the way, how did you manage to get away from the Manor and come down here? Didn't Goodman try to stop you?"

"He didn't know. He left my door unlocked when he went out—I suppose he thought I'd go straight to bed. I saw that it gave me a chance to get away. When I was sure he had rejoined those others, I crept downstairs. I dared not try the front door lest they should hear the hinges creak, so I followed your example." She smiled wanly at Brian. "I got out of the window of one of the ground-floor rooms, and ran here as fast as I could."

Sybil paused, looking from one to the other, her small figure huddled in the big chair. "I'm not going back," she cried suddenly. "If he found out what I'd done, he'd kill me! I'm *never* going back!"

"Of course you aren't," put in Pamela reassuringly. "You're going to stay with us. We'll look after you. Now in exchange for what you've told us," she went on, "you'd better understand the situation here." She went on to speak of the dead telephone and the useless cars, and that Brian was about to go down to the village on foot to ring from the call-box there.

"He'll never reach it—he'll be waylaid!" Sybil exclaimed. "Uncle is taking no chances!"

"That's probable," commented Frank, shifting his plastered arm to a more comfortable position. "Goodman would not forget that call-box, knowing it was pointless to cut our wires and leave the way down to the village open."

"Oh, what are we to do?" cried Sybil.

"If both cars weren't out of action we'd take one of them, and with Brian driving we'd all clear out to a less hectic locality for the night. We'd crash through somehow, even if they did try to hold us up. But as it is——"

Frank broke off abruptly as an idea occurred to him.

"I was about to say," he continued, addressing his three companions, "that as it is, the only choice left seems to be trying to get away on foot and risk being stopped and beaten up—not a cheerful outlook for a party consisting of two girls, a cripple like me, and only one sound man, opposed to four toughs.   But I've remembered something."

The others looked at him expectantly.

"There's an alternative to trying to reach the village call-box," Frank went on.   "Look here, Brian, you know the road over yonder, to the west, and running along the base of the high ground?   In a direct line it's not a lot farther from here than the village is."

Brian nodded.   He remembered seeing below him the lights of passing cars, when on his way to earlier vigils on Black Knapp and skirting the trees which fringed the lip of the drop to the low country. "Well?" he asked.

"If you were to strike out direct from the back of this house, and take a straight line to the nearest trees and down through the woods on the hillside, you'd come to a tiny hamlet.   It's only three or four cottages, but there's a roadside call-box there."

"I'm off, then!" Brian rose to his feet and reached for his torch and borrowed overcoat.   Then he paused.   "I don't altogether like it," he added.   "It means leaving you and the two girls here, and if those swine turn up while I'm away——"

"There's no choice," retorted Frank.   "For heaven's sake get a move on, Brian, and don't waste precious minutes.   The betting is they won't turn up just yet, from what Miss—er—dash it, Sybil—has

13

just told us.   Apparently Goodman hopes to catch us in bed and asleep.   Oh, and one more thing."

"Yes?" said Brian, who was moving off.

"Don't waste time trying to ring Copthorne.   He can be told later.   This is urgent, and it's the county police headquarters you want."

"All right, all right!   Copthorne told me that, and I haven't forgotten," Brian replied huffily, feeling that Frank might have credited him with so much sense, especially considering the way that everything was devolving on himself.

Brian slipped away from the rear of the cottage, crossed the shimmering snow of the neglected garden where the silvered stone of the dovecot rose in the moonlight, and scrambled over the wall beyond.

He headed straight for the line of leafless trees that loomed ahead, anxiety for those he had left spurring him onwards.

Within a few minutes he was beyond the open ground and under the snow-rimmed boughs. Twenty yards farther, and he reached the spot where the hillside began to fall away steeply.

In spite of the need for haste, Brian found he had to ease his pace.   The interlacing branches overhead cut off much of the moonlight, and their shadows cast a confusing pattern on the ground beneath.   He saw at once that it would never do to trip against some unseen root or fallen bough and pitch forward headlong, spraining an ankle or even breaking a leg. The only comfort was that he need not bother about making a noise when treading on dead sticks or forcing his way downwards through brambles and bracken—there was no chance of Goodman and his pals being anywhere within earshot.

Brian was just feeling relieved about this fact when someone spoke suddenly out of the deep shadow cast by a nearby trunk. "Oy! Where be yer off to now?"

Brian gave a startled jump. An instant later he recognised the voice. "Nix!" he ejaculated.

"Ah. It's me. What's the 'urry, mister? Tryin' to catch a train or summat?" Nix stepped out from the shadows. He had a gun under his arm, and bulging side-pockets from which the tail-feathers of a brace of pheasants protruded told their own story.

"The last person I expected to meet," exclaimed Brian. "I couldn't have hoped for anything better!"

"I been 'avin' a change," volunteered Nix. "With this 'ere snow, the open wold ent much cop, but there's allus long-tails a-roostin' in this 'ere wood come night-time. But as I said afore, where be you tearin' off to?"

Remembering Nix's familiarity with the countryside, Brian's first thought was to send him on to the telephone box, but he dismissed it almost at once.

Though Nix might know the ground, he was elderly and a slow mover, and would take longer to reach the spot. Besides, very probably he had never used a telephone in his life, and would muddle things hopelessly. A better use could be made of this chance meeting.

"Look here," said Brian, speaking quickly and urgently, "you remember what I told you last time we met by moonlight in the fields at the foot of Black Knapp?"

"Ah. 'Bout some rogues what you was layin' out for to see, an' Mr. Tilney's accerdent, an' arl that? P'lice job o' sorts."

"Yes. You said you'd help if needed, and the need's urgent now. I can't stop to explain, but go and stand guard at Slad Cottage till I get back. Tilney's helpless with his broken arm, and there's no one to protect him and his sister, or Miss Kelly, who's there too."

"What? That there wench from the Manor? What's she a-doin'——?"

"They'll tell you all about it when you get there. Be as quick as you can, there's a good chap!"

Brian turned to hasten on with his journey.

Nix watched him disappear among the shadows. Then before moving off himself he put down his gun, drew the dead pheasants from his pockets, and carefully hid them under a convenient bramble bush. "Reckon if I'm goin' to get mixed up wi' them there p'lice afore mornin', they'll lay a lot safer there!" he muttered with a grin. "But this 'ere may come in 'andy," he added as he retrieved his gun and trudged off in the direction of Slad Cottage.

Brian no longer felt so anxious about those whom he had left. Nix could be relied upon to put up a good show if there were any developments during his absence.

Stumbling and tripping, Brian made his way downwards. The darkness under the trees seemed endless, and every root and loose stone and trailing bramble seemed to have joined in league to delay him. Roosting birds uttered their protests at the disturbance of their rest, and once some animal scuttled hastily away before his noisy advance, but whether it was a fox or a badger or a stray dog he had no idea. All he cared about was reaching the end of the wood and easier travelling.

At last he saw glimpses of clear moonlight between the trunks. He clambered over a rickety fence and emerged into the open. Ahead a gentle slope merged into the level country.

Brian broke into a run. The reflection of the lights of a passing car told him that he was not far from the road. Those dimmer, stationary gleams to his left front must surely come from the windows of the hamlet which Frank had mentioned. He changed his course slightly, making direct for them. A final gate was surmounted, and his feet were on the black tarmac from which wheels had worn away the covering of snow.

He ran past the first cottage, looking eagerly for the call-box. Just beyond the second building he caught sight of it. Panting, he dived inside, and in the tattered county directory on the shelf began feverishly to look up the required number.

The deep voice of authority answered. Brian gave Copthorne's name as an introduction, and in as few words as possible explained the situation. The duty constable at the other end said he would pass on the message to the right department for immediate action, the tone of his voice showing that he himself knew nothing of any arrangement that might have been made with the London police. He added that no doubt a fast car, well manned, would be on its way to Kinford in a few minutes. "They shouldn't be long, provided they don't stick in a drift somewhere," he ended—words which somewhat damped Brian's spirits. He could have done without that final remark.

As Brian left the telephone box he realised how leg-weary he was. He had covered many miles on foot since the early afternoon when he had set out to procure Pamela's groceries from the village shop.

Nor were his exertions over yet—the homeward ascent had still to be faced.

He turned his back on the little group of cottages and began to retrace his steps. He reached the lower edge of the woods. Coming down through them had been bad enough, but climbing up was far worse.

Every step was a dragging effort, and more than once he fell forward on his face in the snow as his foot caught in some root. Yet he dared not ease off, for every minute increased the possible danger to those who waited at Slad Cottage. Once he was back, Brian felt that with Nix's aid any direct attack might be staved off till the police arrived. Hopefully he thought that if they were quick they might possibly turn up about the same time as he did; but the words of the Gloucester constable, "if they don't stick in a drift", rang their warning in his brain.

Doggedly he clambered upwards. At last he reached the brow, and caught a glimpse of the open wold between the last of the trunks. Brian looked anxiously in the direction of the cottage, but there was no red glow of flames which he had half expected to see. He stumbled onwards at a weary trot, only slowing his pace for the last hundred yards, in case Goodman and his friends might be lurking somewhere in the garden.

Despite his fatigue, as Brian entered the sitting-room the scene there brought a smile to his lips. Nix was sitting self-consciously on the very edge of his chair, looking queerly unfamiliar without his shapeless cap which, with his gun, lay on the carpet beside him. Frank was trying to make conversation and finding it difficult, for the two had little in common and the topic of the moment had long since been exhausted. On the other side of the hearth Pamela was doing her best to take Sybil's mind off the present by trying to interest her in some futile article in a woman's magazine which lay on her knee. As Brian entered, the atmosphere of strain disappeared, and they all turned eagerly towards him.

"That's done!" said Brian as he sank into a vacant seat. "I got through and gave an outline of the situation, and they're sending a car-load of police. They ought to be here any time, but as the chap at the other end warned me, they may get hung up somewhere. I fancy the main roads are fairly clear, but elsewhere there may be drifts."

"Ah, them p'lice never do turn up time 'em's wanted," commented Nix. " 'Tis only when a chap can do without 'em they shows up. Like o' that there Watts," he added, alluding to sundry past contacts with the village constable.

"Well, at least we know they're on the way," replied Brian, "and with you and me here we'll be able to put up a bit of a scrap if things start happening before they arrive. I expect Mr. Tilney has already explained to you how things stand?"

"Ah, 'e 'as, and it's a proper rum-'un for sure. About that there Goodman up at Manor. You could 'a' knock me down with a fevver time 'e tell me. I can't 'ardly believe it now. I don' say it ent right, mind yer; some'ow though Goodman's live in Kinford years an' years, 'e never did seem like o' t'other gentry what lives in big 'ouses round 'ere. Not but what Stan Dawson say 'e's a good master an' knows what's what," Nix added in extenuation.

Silence fell in the room, except for the murmurs of the two girls with their heads together over the magazine.

CHAPTER XVI

RETREAT TO THE DOVECOT

PRESENTLY Nix spoke again.

"Do yer know what?" he asked, addressing the two other men of the party. "I reckon we can do better nor stoppin' 'ere. Too many winders an' doors in this 'ere cottage for my likin'."

"What's the alternative?" responded Frank. "We're better off here than wandering about in the open."

"Ah, I didn't say naught about bein' outside. It's like this 'ere. What about that there old dovecot what's out back there?" Nix jerked a thumb in its direction. "It ent unlike one o' them old-fash'ned castles what yer sees in pictures. Them walls is three foot thick and there ent no winders, and the door was made by folk what knew their job—solid oak, that is, an' barred with iron. Anyone tryin' to get in won' be for shiftin' that in a nurry."

"Not a bad idea!" exclaimed Frank, sitting up abruptly. "Besides, a move will gain time; Goodman and his pals will try getting in here and searching for us, and be wondering where we are when they find we're not in bed. Every minute gained makes it more likely that the police will show up. Come on, let's shift."

The others nodded agreement. Warm clothes were quickly collected, for it was likely to be more than a little chilly in that ancient and unheated building. The lamp was put out, and silently the party left the cottage by the back door.

When all were inside the dovecot, Brian turned the key which he had transferred from the outside of the door. The lower part of the building was pitch dark, but a dim light was visible higher up where the rays of the moon were coming through the apertures by which the doves had once entered. Torches helped the girls up the ladder-like stairs, and empty boxes were brought from the junk-heap to serve as seats for them and for Frank.

Brian and Nix took a quick survey to find out from which loopholes they could obtain the best views of the surrounding area. One or two offered an excellent outlook towards the back of the cottage they had just left, while from another a survey of the slad road could be had.

Silence fell, except for an occasional murmured word between the girls, and the subdued twittering of some disturbed sparrows roosting among the dusty rafters.

"I don' see nor 'ear them p'lice turnin' up in that

there moty-car," remarked Nix presently. "If they was, we'd know time they was still a long way off, night like this."

"Perhaps they've realised that, and are finishing the last bit on foot," suggested Brian. "They won't want to advertise their coming with bright head-lights and a roaring engine, and so give Goodman's lot ample warning."

"Ah," was Nix's only comment. He had little faith in them turning up at all.

Several more minutes passed. Then Brian, who had been looking out of one of the apertures which faced towards the back of the cottage, drew in his breath sharply. A light was moving behind one of the lower windows.

"They've got in!" he whispered to Pamela, who had risen and joined him at the hole. "They must have forced the front door, though I can't imagine how they did so without us hearing them."

"Unless they used a key," said the girl. Then she added quickly, "Very possibly they did. You re-member when we got back from Oxford after seeing Inspector Copthorne we found somebody had been in, using the key that Mrs. Pratley had hidden."

"Yes, but it was still there—it's hanging in the cottage now."

"I know, but isn't it possible that a quick im-pression was taken and a copy made?" retorted

Pamela. "You can be sure that's how it was done."

Gleams of moving light now appeared at the upper windows, passing to and fro. "It's got 'em thoroughly puzzled," commented Brian to his companion at the loophole. "I'll bet they fully expected to find us all in bed and asleep, and can't make out where the deuce we are. There," he added as the faint sound of something being knocked over reached their ears, "they're probably poking round in every cupboard and peering under the furniture. The longer that keeps 'em busy the better for us. If only those police would show up now they'd have 'em perfectly trapped."

Five minutes later the back door slowly opened, exposing the gleam of a torch. Whoever was carrying it, shone it downwards, and then called out to those still within the cottage. The footmarks left by the party crossing over to the dovecot had been spotted, clearly printed in the snow.

Dimly seen figures joined the first man. For a moment they stood, a dark formless group. Then it broke up and the men stepped forward into the moonlight, advancing slowly like dogs following a scent.

Those who watched from the apertures high up in the ancient building knew that zero-hour had come, for the trail would lead the enemy direct to the dovecot.

There was no longer need for concealment, and hailing them might produce a little more delay, for there was still no sign yet of the police arriving. Brian called out through his loophole.

"That you, Goodman? And your friends Budgeon, Milton and Walters as well? Quite a little party to come to do a late call! Be careful you don't fall into that old well—no, I forgot it's been filled in—but there might be other snags around, you know."

As Brian spoke the taunting words, from the aperture alongside, Nix thrust out the muzzle of his gun, and the moonlight glinted on the barrels.

The four men halted. They had reached a spot about halfway between the cottage and the dovecot. Obviously they did not altogether like the look of that projecting shotgun.

"Nice to have seen you all!" jeered Brian. "Sorry we can't offer you a drink, but this is a dry house. Good-bye, and don't slam the gate behind you!"

Quick words passed between those grouped on the path. Brian and his companions had confidently been expected to be found in the cottage, and no plan had been made by Goodman to cover the present situation. He began to give his orders, but the others had spent most of the last couple of hours filling themselves with the Manor whisky and were in an ugly mood. Ignoring what Goodman was saying, Walters shouted, "Come on, chaps, an' cut their blinkin' throats!" and rushed forward.

That was enough for Nix—he promptly let drive. There was a howl from Walters as a number of the pellets struck him, and he sheered off swearing into cover to see what damage he had sustained. The others scattered, and from one of the now crouching figures a tongue of flame leaped out, and a pistol bullet flattened itself against the stonework just below Brian's look-out.

Nix promptly let drive in the direction of the flash with the other barrel, though no answering cry told him that any of the pellets had registered a hit. That second shot brought a protest from Frank—his police training was against the use of firearms except as a last resort. Nix was quite unrepentant, however. "A dose o' Number Six don' kill nobody, though it sting 'im up proper!" he commented with a grin. "Reckon it'll make 'em keep their distance."

Brian backed him up, pointing out that one at least of the enemy, almost certainly Goodman, was armed and had used a weapon. "Besides," he added, "reports carry a long way on a still cold night like this. If Nix bangs off occasionally the police will hear and hurry up, and the noise will bring them direct here instead of wasting time in stalking the empty cottage."

Nix's action had made Goodman pause, but it had

not altered his determination in the slightest. The
fact that those in the dovecot had a gun was annoying but not disastrous. He presumed that it must
have been in the cottage and they had taken it with
them, for he had no idea that Nix had joined the
party, or that Sybil, whom he thought in bed at the
Manor, was there too. Brian knew too much, and
neither he nor Frank and his sister must be in a
position to transmit that knowledge. After all, it
did not matter where they were knocked out; their
bodies could be carried to the cottage, placed on
their respective beds, and the original plan for covering all traces adhered to.

Peering through the moonlight, he saw a way of
reaching the door without coming under fire. If he
and his friends skirted round under cover of the
apple-trees at the back, made a sudden rush for the
dovecot and kept close under its wall, the gun muzzle
could not be sufficiently depressed through those
narrow apertures in the stonework and brought to
bear on them. It would then remain a simple
matter to circle round to the door and break it down.

Goodman wasted no time in carrying out his plan.
Pamela caught sight of the sudden forward rush of
the enemy, but before her call could bring Nix
across the floor to thrust out his gun in a new direction, the attackers were close under the back wall
and safe from any chance of being fired upon. A

few moments later they had worked round and were outside the door.

Goodman studied it. He had not realised that it was so massive a piece of work. Then his quick eyes noticed that there were two keyholes in the solid oak, one big and weather-worn and dating from the same time as the door, and the other newer, smaller, and much nearer the jamb. That meant a new lock had been fitted within recent years to replace the worn-out ancient fastening, and modern workmanship would not have the same strength. It might be possible to force the bolt out of its socket or even smash the lock entirely.

He turned to Budgeon. "Go and fetch the biggest stone you can find off that wall," he said, pointing to that which Nix had been repairing only a few days previously.

"What, me? I ain't lookin' for a dose o' lead in the backside!" was the muttered reply.

Goodman gave him one fierce look. It was enough, and Budgeon obeyed. Nix caught sight of him as he dashed across the open and tried to bring the gun to bear, but the barrels bumped against the side of the loophole and the result was a miss by yards. As he reloaded he saw Budgeon remove one of the largest of the rough blocks forming the coping. "Pinchin' one o' my best crowners what I just put there!" commented Nix wrathfully.

14

Swinging the rock together, Budgeon and Milton drove it with a crash against the door. It stood firm and almost unmarked, for the massive oak was as hard as the iron which bound it. Again and again they repeated the blow. "The lock's giving!" said Goodman encouragingly.

It was. Modern locks are not made to withstand such assaults, and the hasp was bending and tearing out of its socket.

Those inside the building prepared for the final fight. Nix took his stand at the top of the ladder, with Brian beside him holding an axe taken from the dump of garden tools. The others peered anxiously down from behind.

They saw a crack of moonlight appear up the side of the doorpost. The next blow widened it, and with the one that followed the sorely tried lock snapped completely and the heavy oak swung freely back on its massive hinges.

"The first of yer as shoves 'is 'ead in, 'e cops it!" shouted Nix defiantly.

A head did appear, took a quick glance upwards, and was hastily withdrawn just as Nix pulled the trigger. "Now you knows what you'll get!" yelled Nix as the stunning report thundered round the confined space. None of the charge had hit meat, but the shot was followed by confused shouts that made Brian think that someone had been injured.

An instant later he recognised the shouts as not
those of pain but of alarm and warning.   His heart
leaped—the police must have arrived!   With a joy-
ful shout he scrambled down the ladder.   His first
glance through the open doorway showed him both
Budgeon and the pellet-stung Walters on the
ground, each with a burly constable on top of him,
and the others in full flight with uniformed figures
in pursuit.

Nix, Frank, and the girls had hardly emerged also
before Milton reappeared, being towed along in a
grip from which there was no escaping.   Handcuffs
were clapped on the wrists of the three dejected cap-
tives, and the men were thrust inside the now empty
dovecot which would serve as a temporary prison
until they could be taken off to more orthodox
quarters.

Only Goodman remained still at large.   The
sergeant in charge of the party gave his orders
quickly, "You, and you," he said to two of the constables, "go after Thompson and help him to run
down the fourth chap.   Hoskins, you stand guard
at that broken door, and see that those we've got stay
put inside.   And now," he went on, turning to
Brian and his companions, "let's have your account
of what's been happening here."

Brian and Frank stepped forward to speak, while
the girls remained where they were and Nix lurked

shyly in the background.   As briefly and clearly as possible they gave a résumé of the evening's events, together with those that had led up to them. Naturally Copthorne's name was mentioned, also the need to get hold of Goodman, the prime mover of the whole concern and the only one of the four still uncaught at the moment.

"Don't you worry—he won't get far," said the sergeant confidently.   "Since we had your 'phone-call we haven't been asleep, and by the time I and these men of mine started, steps were being taken to plug all likely bolt-holes."

"That's a relief," said Brian, adding that he and his companions had begun to give up hope of the police ever arriving.   "If you'd been a few minutes later we'd have been in the soup!"

"We skidded into a ditch on the icy road," explained the sergeant, "and thought we were never going to get out again.   Still, we did it.   Then as we got nearer we heard distant shots, and just let her out and took the chance of ending upside down! Who was shooting—that chap with the gun?"   He nodded towards the self-effacing Nix.

Frank nodded.   "Yes.   It was only his banging off at them that kept them at bay so long," he replied, giving Nix his due and abandoning his earlier attitude on the subject.   "He stung up one of them—

that chap you've got in there—and that made 'em pause and think."

The sergeant glanced again towards Nix who, seeing attention drawn to himself, was silently stepping back into deeper shadow. "Got a licence to carry that gun of yours?" he called, grinning.

"Ah," replied Nix briefly. The less said the better was his motto when dealing with the police.

"Not for using it in the way you've just been doing though!" chuckled the man in uniform. "Well now," he went on again to Frank and Brian, "those young ladies had better be off to bed, and you as well. It's past midnight. You'll be safe enough now, and I'll be calling on you again in the morning. In the meantime I must be getting along and see about catching this local squire of yours. Goodman, eh?—strikes me Badman is more his tally!"

With a salute to the girls he took himself off, and Brian and his companions returned thankfully to the cottage to put in some much needed sleep. As the sergeant had said, they were safe enough now, with Goodman on the run and fully occupied in trying to make his getaway, and the others of the gang already in custody. Nix had already disappeared in the direction of the village, where his wife had by now resigned herself to the fact that the police must have caught up with her absent husband at last. So they had, but not in the way she thought.

CHAPTER XVII

BACK AT THE MANOR

WHEN the police had appeared on the scene, Goodman had been the first to become aware of the fact. He had not wasted an instant. His promptness gave him a dozen yards' start. He heard the scuffles and cries behind him as Budgeon and Walters were seized, and the pounding feet of the constables starting to give chase to him and Milton.

Though his body was concentrated on the job of covering the ground, his mind was filled with angry surprise at the wholly inexplicable appearance of the police on the scene. How had they possibly got wind of what was afoot? He had taken every precaution against any message being sent through. Had Budgeon blundered over his job with the 'phone wires, or had Carter managed to reach the village call-box in spite of everything? Something had gone wrong, but what, he could not imagine.

These thoughts passed swiftly through his brain, to be followed by the problem of how to get safely out of his present situation. The first thing to be done was to throw off Milton, who was not far behind and running heavily in a way that could be heard a hundred yards. Goodman gave a selfish grunt of relief as he heard a tussle, and the sound of Milton's steps ceased. The capture freed him from the risk that a fellow fugitive entailed.

A small cloud drifted across the moon. Taking advantage of the passing dimness, Goodman doubled as soon as he had scrambled over the next wall. Before the pursuing constable reached it he had doubled again, darting along under the cover of a hedge and some scrubby bushes. Three or four more jinks, and he could no longer hear anyone following. He congratulated himself on throwing them off, at least for the present. He dropped panting into the shelter of a bramble-filled ditch, and swiftly considered his next move.

Quickly he saw that there was only one course to take. He must get back to the Manor before there was time for the police to turn up there. He would be in bed when they arrived and he would see that his butler and housekeeper, and Sybil as well, should have orders to swear that he had been in his room and asleep since 10 p.m.

There was one drawback, of course. That chap Carter would have a different story to tell to the police. He at least had seen him on Black Knapp, though it was doubtful whether he and the others could definitely have recognised him in the dim light during the assault on the dovecot. But what of it? Goodman himself would have three witnesses to say he had never left the house that evening, and against them there would be only Carter's unsupported statement. Who would believe it of a man of his reputation and standing in the county? Proof there would be none, even if the house were searched from attic to cellar; for the instant he was back at the Manor he would take the precaution of destroying that very private ledger in which he kept a record of his illegal activities and payments and receipts.

He had no fear of Budgeon or Walters or Milton giving him away—they would know too well the penalty exacted by others of their kind for "ratting" to the police. And even supposing they did, who would believe them?—three fellows with known criminal records. So with a stroke or two of luck he should be safe enough: there might be suspicion but could be no real proof.

Goodman rose from his ditch and hurried on towards the Manor. The line of the trees surrounding it came in sight. He would reach it by way of the farmyard and the side door through which he had left with those who were now in the hands of the police. Then upstairs and into bed, and with that one small but intimate volume destroyed, there would be no more need to worry.

He passed between the dark cowsheds. As he approached the corner of the house he pulled up short. There were two unexplained and motionless stars of light in the middle of the drive opposite the front door. He side-stepped into the bordering trees and bushes, and drew nearer.

To his alarm he realised that what he had seen was the side-lamps of a stationary car. He became aware also that the front door was open and that the house itself was not in darkness as it should have been. Windows glowed from lights in the rooms behind them.

Now thoroughly apprehensive, Goodman crept closer. The vehicle standing in the drive was definitely a police car, for he could see a uniformed constable sitting at the wheel. A man in a flat cap descended the steps to speak to the waiting driver, and then returned into the house. Through the open hall-door Goodman caught a glimpse of the fat figure of his butler, clad in a dressing-gown and with fright written on his pasty face, being questioned by another policeman. His housekeeper was there also, her hair in curlers, and wearing an expression hardly less perturbed than that of her husband.

It came home fully to Goodman that he was too late, that though one car had gone to Slad Cottage, another had driven direct to the Manor, its action prompted by whatever message Carter had managed to get through.

Goodman saw his old life crashing in ruins. He felt a pang of sincere regret at the thought that he would have to abandon for ever his herd of pedigree cattle, for he had been really interested in them, apart from the fact that they had provided a useful camouflage. And his collection of prehistoric relics —that hobby of his must go too. However, he comforted himself by the recollection that money would be no anxiety; he had ample funds stowed away under different names, both in England and abroad. Moreover, there were plenty of places in which he could disappear, provided he could reach them. In the meantime it was vitally urgent that he should get away at once from the neighbourhood of Kinford.

The problem was to do so without being recognised by the first person he should meet. There was no chance now of getting hold of his car for a quick getaway. Crouching in the bushes by the drive he considered one or two schemes and turned them down. Then a smile spread over his face and he even allowed himself to chuckle under his breath. He rose to his feet, looked round cautiously, and started to make his furtive way in the direction of Kinford village.

In spite of having gone to bed so late, Brian was awake and about at the usual time next morning, eager to find out the latest developments. He and Pamela had their breakfast together, for Frank's arm had been paining him and he was taking it easy, and Sybil was still in the bed which she had shared with Pamela, sleeping the sleep of exhaustion after her recent experiences and worry.

There was a knock at the outer door. Brian rose eagerly to see who was there, expecting it to be last night's sergeant, come for fuller details as he had said he would, and possibly bringing news of Goodman's arrest. Instead he found Detective Inspector Copthorne on the doorstep.

"Oh, hullo!" exclaimed Brian in surprise. "Then you've heard what's been happening here? I tried to ring you, but——"

"I've heard all right," said Copthorne with a smile as he entered. "The county police put through a call to me about 2 a.m. this morning, and I left London an hour later. *Not* a pleasant run, but it's all in the day's—or rather the night's—work. If you've any breakfast going, I shan't say 'No' if you ask me to have some!"

"Rather. Of course. Miss Tilney and I are only just finishing ourselves, and there's plenty. And a good fire for you to get warm by."

While Copthorne ate, at his request Brian went

over the events which had happened since the previous afternoon, and answered an occasional question put to him. At the end, Brian asked one
himself.

"Any news yet of Goodman being caught?"

Copthorne shook his head. "Not that I've heard.
I meant to ring up the county police from here as
soon as I arrived, but your 'phone's dead, you say.
I must see about having it put right. Anyway," he
went on, "the local men are making every effort to
find your friend Goodman. A general warning has
gone out, and all railway stations, ports and airfields
have been notified, in case he's already got away from
this district."

Copthorne paused to lean back in his chair and
light a pipe. "I feel a lot better for that good breakfast you've given me, Miss Tilney. Much more able
now to tackle the next thing."

"Which is?" asked Brian.

"I think a visit to the Manor is indicated. The
local men will have already questioned the house-
hold staff, but there's nothing like having a look
round oneself. By the way, what about that young
woman you mentioned, Goodman's niece? She's
here, I understand?"

"Yes," replied Pamela. "I'm looking after her,
poor girl. She's still asleep at the moment."

"Quite so. Don't disturb her. I shall have to

ask her some questions sometime, but there's no
hurry about that." Copthorne glanced at his watch.
"Now I'll be going. You'd better come along too,"
he added to Brian. "You know the house, which is
more than I do."

Brian and Copthorne went out to the latter's
waiting car. On arrival at the Manor they found a
constable standing near the front door, who said
there was a plain-clothes detective inside the house.
They went in to find him.

They did so in what was obviously Goodman's
study. Amongst other things it contained a large
roll-top desk with a telephone on it. Several farm-
ing papers lay about, and the shelves of the nearby
bookcase bore a number of account books and
various volumes dealing with the management of
livestock.

Copthorne introduced himself, and asked a number of questions, especially if any papers or memo-
randa had been found that might have a bearing on
the case.

The local man shook his head. "Not come on
anything yet," he replied. "Those account books
are exactly what they appear to be—farm records.
I've been through those drawers"—he pointed to
the ones in the lower part of the desk. "Nothing
to interest us there. None of them was locked."

"Any safe? Or strong-room?"

"Nothing of that nature.   The staff say there isn't one, and I believe them, for cheque-book, wages-cash, and all that sort of thing were lying about for anybody to see.   Unless there's a wall-safe cunningly hidden somewhere."

"Looked in Goodman's bedroom?   Sort of place extra private stuff is kept."

"Bare as a monk's cell," replied the plain-clothes man not altogether accurately, for Goodman liked his comfort.

"Looks as if he was too clever a chap to put anything down in writing.   If so, he's an exception; most men of his sort can't resist boasting to themselves on paper."

There was a silence for a moment, which Brian broke.

"What about that museum place?" he asked. "Where Goodman kept his collection of prehistoric relics, I mean.   I know he kept it locked, for he showed it me only yesterday and I noticed he was particular about relocking it after we went out."

"You mean that room upstairs with glass cases full of old stones and bones?" queried the detective. "Yes, I found it locked, but I didn't take long to get in."   He exhibited a bunch of skeleton keys he drew from his pocket.   "Nothing doing there."

"All the same, let's go up and have a look at it," suggested Copthorne.

They did so.   On entering, Brian's glance strayed
to the desk he had noticed before, which seemed out
of place in a room obviously dedicated to its main
purpose.   He commented on the fact.

Copthorne crossed over to it.   "Let's have those
keys of yours for a moment," he said.   Taking them,
he opened the top and began to rout about amongst
the contents.   His hand withdrew a small fat
volume.   He glanced at the hand-written pages, and
gave a whistle of astonishment.

Looking over his shoulder, Brian saw that it was
a carefully kept diary and business record—but not
of the cattle business.   Details of all past robberies
which Goodman had organised were there, each one
headed with the place and date.   The value of the
loot appeared on the credit side, with the outlay involved duly debited on the other, together with notes
about who had been employed to do the job and
comments on the way it had been carried out.   One
of the last entries referred to Romsey.   "Eliminated
this danger," was the terse comment, followed by
the date on which Brian had found the man in the
road.

"Didn't I say clever men can't resist putting things
down on paper?" remarked Copthorne.   "This is
enough to settle Master Goodman's hash as soon as
we've caught him!"   Copthorne placed the little

book in his pocket, and then changed his mind and handed it to the local detective instead.

"I think it would be better if you kept this," he said, "as I shall be on the move.   Guard it carefully until you get back to your headquarters and have it locked up there in the office safe."

"You bet I will!" answered the other with a grin.

CHAPTER XVIII

THE VICAR'S BEST SUIT

WHEN Copthorne was satisfied that there was nothing more of value to be gleaned at the Manor, he and Brian returned to the car and drove slowly away in the direction of Kinford village.

"I've been wondering," Copthorne remarked thoughtfully.

"Yes?" said Brian.

"It's nearly twelve hours since Goodman was last seen, and I understand that since the first streak of daylight patrols have been scouring the countryside. But what was there to prevent him doubling back and finding some hiding-place in the village?"

"I can't think of anyone who would take him in," objected Brian. "And anyone finding himself knocked up at midnight by a person so well known locally as Goodman would immediately smell a rat. We should have heard about it by now—you know what village gossip is."

"Unless that person were a special friend of his, or under some obligation. What about that man Lethwick whom Tilney originally suspected?"

"I very much doubt it," replied Brian.   "He may be a bit of a shady dog from what you discovered, but on the other hand Goodman is very much 'the boss', and I can't see Lethwick taking orders from him. Both too much alike in personality.   I should say their mutual dislike was genuine and not put on."

"Yes, I expect you're right—it was just a passing thought.   At the same time, Goodman may have found some local refuge.   If not, he must be many miles away by now."

The car began to enter the village street.   Copthorne caught sight of a uniformed figure and slowed up.   "Is that your local bobby?" he asked, and when Brian replied that it was, added, "I think I'll have a chat with him."

P.C. Watts appeared to be somewhat embarrassed at finding himself being consulted by "an officer of the Yard" as he understood Copthorne to be, for of course he had heard of his arrival—nothing ever happened in Kinford but that it was universally known in half an hour.

Copthorne asked various questions about the village and its people that seemed to Watts to have no bearing whatever on the affair that was thrilling the neighbourhood.

"No, sir," he replied to another apparently pointless query, "all the folks here are usually in bed before nine, and it's the rarest thing to see a light in

a window later than nine-thirty.   Barrin' o' course,
the Vicarage," he added as an afterthought.   "The
Reverend Quaintance, he don' seem to go to bed at
all—he sit up porin' over books.   Many a time I've
seen his light burnin' in his study as late as two in
the mornin', time I've been on my way home after
doin' a night beat."

"Bit of a scholar, eh?"

"Yes, sir.   Thass all about he do do, you might
say.   More'n once a young couple's been waitin' at
the church to be married, or a funeral to be took,
and he's forgot all about it and had to be fetched!"

Copthorne laughed, dismissed the constable with
a nod, and turned the car.   "I think we'll call on
this vicar," he said to Brian.   "That's the house, I
take it, next to the church.   I wonder why nearly
all vicarages have dismal laurels growing in front of
them; they must cut off half the daylight from the
lower windows."

Mr. Quaintance was a widower, and his housekeeper, a person as dismal as the laurels, answered
the call of the old-fashioned jangling bell which
Copthorne had pulled.   Yes, the Vicar was in his
study, she said, in a tone that implied he was never
anywhere else, and showed them in.

Mr. Quaintance rose politely to greet his visitors
and held out a vague hand.   They introduced themselves, but the words obviously did not penetrate,

any more than had Frank's account of how he had come by his injury when the Vicar had called at Slad Cottage to enquire.

Not very hopefully, Copthorne asked his host if he had seen Goodman recently.

The Vicar's brow furrowed in thought. "No, I don't think so. Nice fellow, but I don't often meet him. He lives up at the Manor, you know—if you want to see him you'll find him there, I've no doubt."

He alone of the whole district knew nothing of recent events!

"You didn't by any chance see him last night?" Copthorne persisted. "I understand you were sitting up late as usual."

"I expect I was. I was deep in a new commentary on St. Paul's Epistle to the Ephesians, and I remember I got quite annoyed with some of the author's arguments. Now that's odd!—speaking of that commentary reminds me that I *did* see Goodman. It must have been well after midnight when he interrupted my reading."

Copthorne felt the same thrill as a hunter who picks up the trail of a beast he is following. "Quite so," he said. "Can you remember what he wanted?"

"Yes, it was rather peculiar now I come to think of it. I heard a tap at the window. I thought it was just a laurel branch—they ought to be cut back. I must see to it, but I can't afford a regular gardener and the lad who comes twice weekly from the village is not as energetic as he might be. These young people nowadays never seem to——"

"You say you heard a tap at the window?" interrupted Copthorne firmly.

"Oh yes, that is so, and it occurred to me that someone must be outside. I opened the sash and Goodman climbed in. He looked quite queer, and his usually smart clothes were all torn and stained. In fact I remarked on them and he promptly asked if he could borrow some of mine to go home in."

"And you lent him some?" prompted Copthorne, for the Vicar had paused and his glance had strayed back to the book he had been reading.

"I believe I did—he seemed so insistent. I remember saying, 'Take your choice, my dear fellow, as long as you don't expect me to go and fetch them. Upstairs, first door on the right, is my room,' I said, and that was the last I saw of him. I suppose he went out some other way. I expect he'll return anything he borrowed in a day or two."

"Thank you very much for what you've told me," said Copthorne. "You've helped a lot."

"Have I? I'm sure I don't know how, but I'm always glad to be of assistance. Are you going? Won't you both stay and have something—coffee or tea or a glass of lemonade?"

Copthorne and Brian excused themselves, and

turned to the door. Before they had closed it behind them the Vicar was once more bending over his book.

"What a fellow!" said Copthorne as the two left the house.

"Goodman or the parson?" said Brian with a grin.

"The parson, of course. And Goodman, too, if it comes to that, but in a different way. He was smart enough to guess that our clerical friend would forget all about his midnight visit, and what better disguise could he adopt than that of a clergyman's black clothes and conventional 'dog-collar'?"

"Which means that he's certainly no longer in this neighbourhood," said Brian.

"Exactly. Round here a strange parson would be spotted at once, whereas in a town nobody would take any notice. What we've now got to puzzle out is not so much where he's gone but how he went. Not on foot, I imagine, yet we've had no report of a car or a bicycle having been stolen from its sleeping owner. There's no railway station for miles. Are there any early buses running here?"

"Not that I know—never seen a bus in Kinford at all," replied Brian. "But we can ask Watts."

"Good idea. He has given us one good tip, and may be able to produce another."

They found the village constable at his cottage.

"No, sir, there ent no bus service here at all, much

less an early one," he replied to Copthorne's question. "The only bus travellin' anywhere near is Barton's, but that passes two miles away." P.C. Watts went on to explain that the vehicle came daily from a market town situated on the main road that ran along the base of the high ground, and did a sort of circular tour of the wolds picking up workmen, and another trip in the evening dropping them again near where they lived.

"What time does it pass the turn leading to Kinford?" asked Copthorne.

"About 7.40 maybe, sir—when it's hardly light this time o' the year."

"Is this bus owner, Barton, on the 'phone?"

"I dunno, but I expect he is, sir. Runs a garridge, he does, so it's likely."

"I'll ring him up at once. Got a 'phone here?"

Watts shook his head. "No, sir, there ent been one put in. If I want to make a call I has to go to the public box up-street."

"Then I'll have to use that. Come on, Carter," Copthorne added to Brian, "the sooner we get in touch with this man the better. He may give us a clue that will take us another step forward."

Copthorne found the required number in the usual tattered directory which such places contain, and got through. "That Mr. Barton?" he asked. "This is a police call—Detective Inspector Cop-

thorne speaking. I want to have a word with the
man who drove your early workman's bus this morning."

"I drove her meself—I always does," came the
reply. "What's the trouble? Everythin's been done
proper an' all that."

"I've no doubt that is so. What I want to ask
you is this. When you passed the turn nearest to
Kinford this morning, did you by any chance pick
up a clergyman there?"

"Well, it's a rum-'un you should ask that, mister,
for happen I did pick up a parson chap standing
alongside of the couple o' men what waits there
usual. Got a muffler round his face against the cold,
an' a black hat pulled down. He wasn't the sort o'
passenger I often gets, not at that time o' the mornin'
when it's hardly light, so I notices him particular.
Parsons ent ones for gettin' up early, not by a long
chalk. What's he been doin'? Pinchin' the collection?" Barton added with a chuckle.

"Never mind about that now," retorted Copthorne. "Where did he get off?"

"Why, at the same stop where I set down all the
rest of 'em—in the market-place here."

"Did you see which way he went then?"

"Not particular. But he did ask me where he
could catch a bus for Cheltenham, and I told him

there'd be one along in a few minutes.   There's a reg'lar service along that main road."

"Thanks a lot—you've been very helpful."

"That's O.K. as long as I ent wanted as a witness in a court case—I'm a busy man, I am, an' got no time to waste."

"You needn't be afraid of that.   G'bye!"

Copthorne rang off and left the box.   He reported to Brian what Barton had replied.   "I'll be off at once to Cheltenham to see if I can pick up the trail there, and as I've no time to run you back to Slad Cottage, do you mind if I leave you to walk home?"

"Not in the slightest."

"Right.   There's nothing more you can do at present, but if I get on Goodman's trail I shall most probably need you again.   You see, I don't know the man by sight, but you do and will be able to identify him at once.   And now I'm off—good-bye for the present."

With these words Copthorne restarted his engine and drove away.

He was in a hurry, but not to the extent of risking a smash.   With the pounding-down of the snow by traffic, the roads had become very slippery, and only in a few places had they been gritted.   Keeping a steady pace he covered the distance without mishap, and on reaching Cheltenham went first to the offices of the bus company.

In reply to his enquiry he was told that the conductor of the bus which Goodman had most probably caught was away on another journey, but was
due back shortly. Copthorne waited. When at last
contact was made the conductor said he remembered
a man in parson's clothes boarding his vehicle at the
spot referred to, and getting off at a bus-stop in the
centre of the town.

Copthorne felt that that was one more point
gained. Goodman had not gone on to the bus-park
from which many other routes radiated, and the
chances were therefore that he was still in Cheltenham. The inspector's next port of call was the head
police station, where he introduced himself and
explained the reason for his visit. He found the
county police only too eager to co-operate. He put
forward the theory he had formed.

"It looks to me as if Goodman intends to find a
hide-out in this town and lie low until he's worked
out his plans for the future," Copthorne suggested.
"He will avoid going to any big hotel, and probably
keep clear of small ones too; his most likely choice
would be to pick some rather obscure boarding-
house. Now you know where these places are.
Can you send round and find out from various land-
ladies if a recently-arrived parson has engaged a
room with them?"

"It's a big job," he was told. "Cheltenham's as

full of boarding-houses, and people who let lodgings, as currants in a cake.   We can do no more than our best.   We'll detail the men at once and give them their instructions, but it's likely to be a bit of time before we get hold of anything useful . . ."

CHAPTER XIX

ON THE ROOFS

IT was not long after Brian had left with Inspector Copthorne for the Manor, that Sybil came downstairs. Though she had slept well, she was considerably worried about her future after what had happened. The fact showed in her face, and Pamela guessed the cause. She broached the subject as soon as the girl had finished her breakfast.

"You're stopping here with us just for as long as you like," she assured her guest. "But at the same time you ought to know how you stand—financially, I mean. Brian mentioned to me that you'd told him you had money in trust; have you any idea who the trustees are, and all that?"

"No, I haven't," Sybil admitted. "All I know is that the income went to my uncle—to cover my keep," she added with a touch of bitterness in her voice.

"Isn't there *anyone* you can think of? Didn't your parents have a lawyer who did things for them?"

"Oh yes." Sybil mentioned his name. She added

an address, saying, "I think that's where he lived, though I may not have got it quite right."

"Telephone number?" asked Pamela briskly.

Sybil shook her head.

"No matter, I'll get it out of 'Enquiries'. The sooner we get in touch with him the better, as very probably he'll know all about your affairs. I wonder if the 'phone is working again." Pamela rose and crossed over to the instrument.

To her surprise it was, for a few minutes earlier Budgeon's device for short-circuiting the wires had been spotted, and removed by an agile policeman.

After some difficulty she made contact with the lawyer, but not unnaturally found him sticky. Defeated in getting any information herself, she pulled Sybil over to the receiver to have a try. Luckily the man at the other end had a good memory for voices, and became more communicative. He expressed his horror at the turn of events in the matter of Goodman, but assured Sybil that her capital was safe and advised her to come up to London and see him as soon as possible.

When Brian returned after having been dropped in the village by Copthorne, he found Sybil in a much happier mood. Her affairs were discussed, and the matter of finding a job later was gone into. Brian promised that when he himself returned to London he would do his best to find some opening which she could fill, despite her lack of any training.

As Brian spoke of his return, it reminded him that his holiday at Kinford was drawing to a close. Only two or three days remained of his leave, and then he would have to go back to work.

Would Copthorne, he wondered, catch up with Goodman before the time that remained had expired? Copthorne had said he would need him and send for him, and Brian felt that it would be tough luck, after all he had done, if he were to miss the final scene.

The day passed without news, nor was there any next morning. Then about eleven o'clock the telephone rang. Pamela, who was nearest, answered it, and then beckoned to Brian. "For you," she said. "It's Inspector Copthorne, speaking from Cheltenham."

Brian sprang across the room and took the receiver from Pamela's hand.

"I want you to come along right away," said the voice at the other end. "The local police have been combing the town for possible suspects in clerical clothes putting up at boarding-houses. They have located four whom I want to interview, and I need you with me to identify Goodman. Is your car in order again?"

"Yes, a mechanic was sent out with a new rotor. She's going well now."

"Right. Come at once, then. Meet me outside the main police station here." There was a click at the other end as Copthorne rang off.

Brian wasted no time in getting started. The weather had turned milder, and except for slush in places the roads were clear of snow, though it still lay in dirty heaps under the hedges and walls. He was able to drive fast, therefore, and did not take long to reach his destination.

"Glad you've been prompt," was Copthorne's greeting. "Leave your car—a constable will run it into the yard at the back." He signed to Brian to enter a waiting police car, and followed himself. The uniformed driver started his engine, and they moved off.

"As I told you, I have four addresses at which to call," said Copthorne. "We will take them in turn, beginning at the nearest."

Brian nodded. Then a thought crossed his mind. "Did you find any firearms on Budgeon and the other two when they were caught?" he asked.

Copthorne smiled. "I can guess what you are thinking. That it was Goodman who fired back that night of the attack on the dovecot, and that he's probably still got the weapon on him. Budgeon and Co. had empty pockets, and we haven't forgotten that fact." He made a gesture to the rear.

Brian glanced out of the back window. Another

car was following at a discreet distance. Armed help
would be quickly available if needed.

The driver drew up at the first house on the list.
The clergyman who was putting up there was certainly not Goodman—he was a country rector and
had chosen to lodge with an old parishioner rather
than go to some impersonal and much more expensive hotel. Copthorne apologised for disturbing
him, and the car moved on to the next address.

Here they found that the man in question was out,
but from the landlady's description he was a young
curate who had just been appointed as assistant at
a nearby church. Copthorne ticked him off the list,
and once more the journey was resumed.

The next port of call was at one of a terrace of
tall Regency houses, once part of a fashionable
quarter but now sunk a long way down the social
scale. The word "Apartments" appeared behind
most of the fanlights, and the steps and porticoes
were cracked.

A stout and breathless female, wearing a by no
means incipient moustache, appeared in answer to
the ring on the bell.

"Yes," she admitted, "I've a clerical gent here—
he came two days back. I could only offer him my
top room—it ain't much of a place, bein' little
more'n an attic—but with this conference of the New
Song-Writers, whatever they is, at the Baptist Hall

at the end o' the street, I was full up, see? You wants to speak to the gent? Well, maybe he's still in his room. He tole me he was leavin' 'safternoon, and he's paid what he owes, but I don' expect he's gorn yet."

"Top room, you say? Then we'll find it. Don't bother to show us the way," said Copthorne.

"Ah, that'll save me legs—I've enough runnin' about to do, and I ain't as young as what I was. Right up the stairs it is, and on the top landin' you'll see a door to the left."

Copthorne swiftly ascended the stairs, with Brian close behind him. They reached the door. "When the man comes, if it's Goodman say 'Yes'," Copthorne whispered, and then knocked.

Both waited tensely. The door opened a few inches and part of a face appeared.

"Yes!" said Brian swiftly.

Goodman was equally prompt in recognising Brian. Before Copthorne could thrust in a foot, the door had been slammed and the key turned.

Both flung their weight against it. The lock was certainly not contemporary with the house, but a cheap mass-produced affair; at the second assault it snapped and the door went back on its hinges. Copthorne and Brian sprang in—to find the room empty!

"That's the way he's gone!" exclaimed Copthorne,

16

pointing to an open skylight and a table hastily pulled beneath it.

Goodman had not seized upon that line of flight without forethought. During a stroll after dark on the previous evening round the back of the terrace, by the light of the street lamps he had noticed that there was a zigzag iron fire-escape ladder descending the building about halfway along its length. His intention was to reach it by way of the roofs, dash down it, and throw off pursuit in the maze of side streets to the rear.

Meanwhile Copthorne had leaped upon the table. Clutching the edge of the skylight frame, he pulled himself upwards. As soon as he was clear, Brian followed him.

They found themselves looking out over an area of slanting slates, gullies and chimneys. The slopes of the roofs were not steep, but Brian felt it was not a pleasant spot on which to conduct a chase, for on the outer side only a coping three or four inches high divided the eaves from a drop of sixty feet to the pavement below. Copthorne had not hesitated, however, and with his heart in his mouth Brian had no choice but to carry on.

Goodman was progressing swiftly ahead of them, making for a definite point. They saw him stop suddenly and make a gesture of baffled fury. He had discovered, what he had not seen in the dim light of the street lamps on the previous evening, that the fire escape did not rise as high as the roof. It ended two storeys down and was impossible to reach, and to attempt to drop in the hope of grasping the iron steps as he fell would be suicidal.

Goodman turned, scrambled up the slates again, and took cover behind a chimney stack. He peered round the side of it at those who were advancing slowly towards him. A sharp report rang out, and a bullet smashed a slate close to Brian's head. So Goodman was armed all right, Brian reflected as he ducked.

The sound of the pistol-shot had its effect; the car which had been following at a distance along the street below accelerated quickly. Uniformed constables came bounding up the stairs to the consternation of the stout and hirsute landlady. One after another they tumbled out on to the roofs and advanced in open order.

Goodman fired another shot. It was promptly answered by one of the armed police.

Goodman broke cover, ran along a gully between two slopes, and scrambled up to where another chimney afforded protection. From his new position he fired again, and one of the policemen made a convulsive clutch at his arm.

The cordon began to close in. Goodman saw it, and moved again, exposing himself. A shot rang out, aimed intentionally low, and wounded him in the leg. He cried out, stumbled, and fell. Clutching desperately to stop his progress, he slithered down the slates.

They offered no grip whatever. He continued to slide towards the eaves above the street, and struck the low coping. It was not enough to check his falling weight. With a despairing cry he disappeared from the sight of those on the roof, and a couple of seconds later they heard the gruesome thud of his body striking the pavement sixty feet below.

Those on the roof turned as one man, and without speaking moved back towards the trapdoor from which they had emerged. With Copthorne leading, and Brian close behind him, they descended the stairs and filed out, ignoring the clamour of the landlady who had recovered sufficiently from her surprise to demand aggressively what the police thought they were doing, bursting like that into an honest woman's house.

The wounded constable was helped into one of the cars and driven off to have his arm seen to, while the other policemen waited for the arrival of a van to remove what lay on the pavement.

"Probably what has happened was the best for everybody concerned," commented Copthorne to Brian as they, too, lingered. "He would have got

twelve or fifteen years, I should say, even if the actual
killing of Romsey could not have been brought
home to him, seeing that the only evidence we have
is what his niece told you, and the entry we found
in the diary."

The van came, and left with its burden.

"Now about yourself," Copthorne went on.
"The job's finished as far as you are concerned, and
I expect you will be wanting to get back to Kinford."

"Yes, I suppose so," said Brian, feeling rather flat
after the excitement of the last half-hour.

Copthorne nodded towards the car which had
brought them to the spot. "We'll be getting back
to the police station where you left yours."

They reached it, and got out. Copthorne held
out his hand. "We owe you a big debt, Carter. If
you hadn't got on to that meeting-place, we might
never have known who was at the bottom of all this
business we've been up against. Good-bye for the
present, and good luck."

Brian turned his car into the road that led back
to Kinford.

As he drove slowly along the village street he saw
Lethwick approaching, presumably out for an afternoon stroll and looking for someone to lecture. He
held up his hand imperiously as he recognised
Brian's car.

"Well, he's got it, I hear—I told ya he would,"

said Lethwick with satisfaction as Brian pulled up.

"Who's got it?" countered Brian, knowing that the news about Goodman could not possibly have reached the village yet.

"Why, that fellar I spoke to ya about, a week or ten days ago; that jumped-up chap who accosted me in that tea-shop on the same afternoon that Tilney and yaself were there. I gave him a talking-to—I told him where he'd land up if he didn't look out, and I was right, ya see! I spotted his kind—a thorough wrong-'un!"

"I've known that for some time," said Brian quietly, his hand on the gear-lever. He had no wish to remain indefinitely in the middle of the road while Lethwick held forth.

"Ya have, have ya? Then I suppose ya thought I was a pal o' his, hey?"

"Well, it did occur to me," Brian could not help saying.

"Oh, so ya did, hey? That's where ya young fellers go wrong. Jump to conclusions—think ya know. Wait till ya get to my age——"

Brian felt no inclination to wait at all. In reply he let in the clutch and the car began to move, leaving Lethwick staring after it, indignant at the way his oration had thus been abruptly cut short.

CHAPTER XX

KNOCK AT THE DOOR

SUPPER that evening at Slad Cottage was a more cheerful meal than many which had been eaten recently, despite the grim tragedy which Brian had witnessed. The feeling of strain had disappeared, and Frank was more himself again owing to the knowledge that it would not be long now before he would have the burdensome plaster removed from his arm.

Sybil also had anxiety lifted from her shoulders. Her uncle's end, though somewhat of a shock, had little effect on her spirits; even before she had found out his true character, she had grown to dislike and fear his domineering ways. She felt that the past lay behind, and ahead was the prospect of a much more free life. It had been arranged that Brian was to drive her up to Town on the following day, when his holiday ended, and drop her at the lawyer's office. Whether she returned temporarily to Slad Cottage or remained in London depended on the outcome of that interview.

A knock reached the ears of the four seated at the

table. "Who on earth can that be?" exclaimed Pamela. "Someone at the back door." She rose and went to find out.

She returned a minute later, ushering in no less a person than Nix. But it was a Nix transformed. He wore his "Sunday suit", in which he was hardly ever seen, and had obviously set out with the intention of paying a formal call. Pamela waved him to a chair, but Nix shook his head.

"Thanky, miss, but I ent stoppin'. I reckoned I'd jest come along an' find out the rights on it. It's arl over the village as 'ow them there p'lice 'ave caught up wi' Goodman, an' killed 'im dead. What's the truth on it?"

"He's dead, sure enough," said Brian, "but it was more an accident than anything else. I was there, and saw the whole thing." He went on to describe how Goodman had been located in a lodging-house, been chased over the roofs, and had fallen to his death in the street.

"Ah!" commented Nix when Brian ceased speaking. "Goodman, 'e wor a rogue, there ent no gettin' away from it, but 'e worn't a bad sort o' chap, come to think on it. Now if it 'ad been that there Lethwick——"

Nix paused, checking himself in an urge to spit. Brian grinned. "You're not the only one to dis-

like him—he stopped me this afternoon in the
village and started to give me quite a lecture."

"Did 'e now?   I runned into that there Lethwick
'safternoon too, a-comin' up street with a cigar as
big as an 'edgestake stickin' out o' 'is face.   'E start
talking about them blokes what's bin shove in
prison, them what I shot at back o' here, an' do yer
know what 'e say then?"   Nix paused again for
effect.

"No—what?" prompted Frank.

" 'E says 'e wonders why a good-for-nothin'
poacher ent bin shove in along o' them—me! what's
bin 'elpin' the p'lice!   But I shuts 'im up quick."
Nix winked at his audience.   "I says to 'im I 'ad a
letter only 'smornin', typewrote an' all, from the
head p'lice boss at Gloucester, a-thankin' me for
what I done.   'An' that's more'n you ever ''ad,' I
says.   Oh-ah, 'e look proper old-fashioned at me
then!"

A laugh sounded round the room, in which Nix
joined.

"Well, I reckon I'll be movin' on.   'Ope I didn't
take the liberty, comin'."   Nix turned to Brian.
"Mrs. Pratley she tell me you're off back to Lunnon
termorrer?"

"Yes, I've got to get back to work."

"Ah, but reckon you done some work 'ere too,
since time you come.   I'll be wishin' yer good-bye,

then." Nix held out a horny hand, which Brian grasped. "Don' you go to forget us, mister—we've 'ad some fun together over them varmints. I laughs now time I thinks o' the way you jump that evenin' you was comin' off Black Knapp and sees me sudden-like. Time the summer come, you wants to 'ave another 'oliday 'ere."

"And I second that motion," said Pamela with a smile as the back door closed behind Nix. "We may not be here all the time, for Frank will be returning to his job, but we'll be at Slad Cottage off and on. At least I shall. So whenever you get time off, and feel inclined to come, let us know."

"Rather! You bet I will," replied Brian with an emphasis that made Pamela blush and then kick herself mentally, knowing that she had done so.

PRINTED FOR THE PUBLISHERS BY
WILLIAM CLOWES AND SONS LTD, LONDON AND BECCLES
85.357